Jet went silent at the mention of his brother's name.

In thinking about Holly's past, he kept overlooking the Cody factor. He pushed his empty plate to the side. Clara took the moment to yawn.

Holly shifted the baby. "I'd better take her home."

"What if I warmed a bottle for you?" he asked. "Would you stay awhile?"

Surprise flickered in her eyes. "You need your sleep. Aren't you getting up in a few hours?"

"I can never sleep the first couple nights of calving. So please stay." Jet tilted his head and shrugged. "Distract me from the cows. I like hearing about your life."

"You do?" Holly ducked her chin briefly. "If you really want me to."

He did. He found himself wanting to know everything there was to know about her. Even if it meant hearing about her life with Cody. Maybe it would help the facts sink in—Holly had loved his brother. There was no place in her heart for Jet...

Jill Kemerer writes novels with love, humor and faith. Besides spoiling her minidachshund and keeping up with her busy kids, Jill reads stacks of books, lives for her morning coffee and gushes over fluffy animals. She resides in Ohio with her husband and two children. Jill loves connecting with readers, so please visit her website, jillkemerer.com, or contact her at PO Box 2802, Whitehouse, OH 43571.

Books by Jill Kemerer

Love Inspired

Wyoming Ranchers

The Prodigal's Holiday Hope
A Cowboy to Rely On

Wyoming Sweethearts

Her Cowboy Till Christmas
The Cowboy's Secret
The Cowboy's Christmas Blessings
Hers for the Summer

Wyoming Cowboys

The Rancher's Mistletoe Bride
Reunited with the Bull Rider
Wyoming Christmas Quadruplets
His Wyoming Baby Blessing

Visit the Author Profile page at LoveInspired.com for more titles.

A Cowboy
to Rely On

Jill Kemerer

LOVE INSPIRED

INSPIRATIONAL ROMANCE

LOVE INSPIRED®

INSPIRATIONAL ROMANCE

Recycling programs
for this product may
not exist in your area.

ISBN-13: 978-1-335-56745-1

A Cowboy to Rely On

Copyright © 2021 by Ripple Effect Press, LLC

This edition published by arrangement with Harlequin Books S.A.

For questions and comments about the quality of this book, please contact us
at CustomerService@Harlequin.com.

Love Inspired
22 Adelaide St. West, 40th Floor
Toronto, Ontario M5H 4E3, Canada
www.LoveInspired.com

Printed in U.S.A.

This I know; for God is for me.
—*Psalm* 56:9b

To Olivia. It's been a joy watching you become an adult. You've worked hard, dealt with adversity, chosen kindness and refused to let life get you down. I'm proud you're my daughter.
I can't wait to see where life takes you!

Chapter One

This wasn't Jet Mayer's first wild-goose chase, but he hoped it would be his last.

The four-hour drive to Cheyenne from Mayer Canyon Ranch in Sunrise Bend, Wyoming, had steeled his resolve even as it sent his nerves into hyperdrive. After parking his truck in the lot of a small apartment complex, Jet cut the engine and got out, bracing himself against the bitter winds. The mottled-gray sky cast a pallor over the scene. February was a dreary month. Matched his dreary mood.

He needed answers about Cody.

His youngest brother's death a year ago had affected the entire family in ways Jet couldn't fully grasp. Questions had been tumbling through his mind since they'd buried his brother, and one full year hadn't quieted them. One of those questions wouldn't leave him be, no matter how many times he tried to push it away.

Who was the mystery woman who'd snuck into the back of the church right before the funeral only to vanish moments later?

She'd been wearing his grandmother's ring. The ring Grandma had given to Jet before her death three years ago. The one he'd realized was missing a few months before the car accident that took Cody's life.

What exactly had his brother been doing down here in Cheyenne besides working as a highway maintenance assistant?

With long strides, Jet headed to the shabby building. Taking the metal stairs two at a time, he then strode down the walkway in search of apartment 205.

This was stupid. The person living here wouldn't know his brother.

Maybe Cody's boss was wrong. Yesterday, Jet had called him and found out Cody had changed his address a few days prior to his death. Didn't make sense since all his stuff had been at the apartment Jet and Blaine had cleared out the day before the funeral.

Should he even bother knocking? He'd taken precious time off from the ranch to drive here. The least he could do was find out if the tenant knew his brother.

Cody could have decided to split an apartment with a coworker or friend and hadn't gotten around to moving his stuff. It was a long shot, but at this point, Jet had nothing to lose. He was in the dark about the final six months of Cody's life. And he took full blame for it.

He'd been too hard on him.

Jet gave the door three sharp knocks. Blew into his cupped hands as the cold air seeped under his coat collar. Rustling sounds came from behind the door. His heart pounded. The door opened…

Her.

The mystery woman. Still wearing Grandma's ring. *His* ring.

His lungs seized as her blue eyes widened, her face draining of color. Her shallow intake of breath told him she was as shocked as he was. He didn't have time to consider the reason because her body collapsed like an inflatable with a sudden leak.

Jet burst into action, thrusting his arms out to catch her before she hit the floor. Instinctively, he swooped one arm under her legs and carried her inside, using his foot to gently kick the door shut behind him. A living room was to his right, and he deposited her on the couch.

A gurgling sound alerted him they weren't alone. A baby was strapped into one of those bouncy chair contraptions.

A baby. He eased his way toward it. The child wore pink pajamas and threw her arms out as she kicked her tiny feet, causing the chair to bounce. She had fine brown hair and round cheeks. She stuck out her tongue and made the chair bounce again.

"What happened?" The woman on the couch sounded groggy as she tried to sit up.

"Easy there," he said. "Take it slow. You fainted."

The confusion clouding her eyes cleared, and she shot to a seated position. Lurching to her feet, she stumbled to the baby, unbuckled the strap and cradled the child to her shoulder as if Jet were a kidnapper or something. Wild-eyed, she patted the baby's back, not taking her gaze off him.

"Are you Cody's brother?" Her voice reminded him of ice-cold lemonade on a hot summer day. Refreshing, sweet and tart. Very tart.

"Yes, I'm Jet Mayer." He took off his cowboy hat and held it between his hands as he fought the urge to shift his weight. "Who are you?"

"Holly Mayer." She didn't blink. Didn't smile. Just gripped the baby. "Cody's wife."

Cody's wife? What wife? His brother could *not* have gotten married without telling the family. Jet crushed the hat in his hands.

"This is Clara. Our baby."

Our baby. The two words repeated over and over in his mind, giving him a dizzy sensation.

Cody had a baby.

Clara was Jet's niece.

How had this happened? Why didn't he and his parents and siblings know about them?

"I see." He didn't, though. He didn't see at all. If Cody had gotten married, Jet and Blaine would have been in the wedding. Dad and Mom would have been told. Erica and Reagan would have helped plan it. There would have been bridal showers and rehearsal dinners and tux rentals and…

Had Cody hated them all so much he'd gotten married behind their backs?

A prolonged hacking cough caught his attention. The woman—Holly, was it?—appeared to be sick. Now that he was getting a good look at her, he noted the dark gray crescents under her eyes, the red nose, pale skin and overall frail appearance.

"Want me to take the baby so you can sit?" He wasn't sure what else to do. Wasn't too familiar with little kids. But Holly looked ready to keel over.

"No," she snapped, clutching the baby tightly. Then she looked back at the couch and lowered herself onto it. And started coughing again.

"Can I at least get you a glass of water?"

She hesitated then nodded as the baby began to fidget. A half wall topped with a counter separated the kitchen from the living area, so he headed toward it. Opened two cupboards before finding the glasses. Ran the tap for a few seconds and filled a glass.

Cold, hard reality was beginning to sink in. Holly and Clara were family. He'd have to introduce them to everyone. From the looks of it, they weren't doing so well. It wasn't just her cough; it was this place. The carpet had bare spots, the walls hadn't been painted in years, and the outdated appliances and chipped cabinets looked to be older than she was. A barking dog next door proved the walls were paper-thin.

He stood at the sink, trying to take it all in, and realized he'd been handed another responsibility. Two, to be exact.

And he was full up on those right now.

Muffled coughing set his feet in motion. He hurried back to her, handing her the glass of water. Her eyes held a gleam of gratitude as she took it and sipped. She shifted the baby in her arms to face him, and the girl's cheerful face took some of his pain away. He could see Cody in her eyes and eyebrows. They looked a lot like his own.

"She's cute." He couldn't help but smile. "You said her name's Clara?"

Holly nodded.

"How old is she?" He had a million more questions, but he'd start there.

"Almost four months."

"And she's my brother's." He didn't question it. It was just hard to take in.

"Yes." Her eyebrows drew together. "Why? Don't you believe me?"

"I believe you. She has the Mayer eyes." He gestured to a worn chair. "May I?"

"Yes."

"You've got the advantage on me." He figured he might as well be honest. "I didn't know Cody got married. I certainly didn't know he had a kid. This is all new, and I don't know what to think."

"I know the feeling."

"You do?"

"Until Cody died, I had no idea he had a family." Her voice was raspy. She took another sip. "He told me he was an only child. An orphan."

A horse could kick him square in the chest and it wouldn't hurt this bad. He tried to fight the pain, but it spiraled through him.

His baby brother had disowned them all. Gotten married and told this woman he had no family.

Man, that stung.

After all they'd done for the kid. After all he'd put them through.

Jet balled his hands into fists. When he thought

about what Cody's death had done to their father, how it had changed each one of his siblings, he wanted to yank his brother out of the grave and yell at him. Didn't he know how much they'd all loved him? How much they'd wanted to be a part of his life? But he'd slammed the door on them, hotheaded and impulsive as ever.

Hot rage pressed tears against the backs of his eyes. Cody had pretended they didn't exist.

Brother, I carried you almost a mile the day you broke your collarbone when you were eight. I mediated between you and Dad when you got caught drinking at fifteen. I was the one who loaned you money to start competing in rodeos. And this is how much I meant to you? I would have done anything for you.

Why was he surprised, though? He'd been the one who'd told Cody the last time he'd seen him that if he wanted to waste his life, he had to do it somewhere else. They'd parted on bad terms. Both too stubborn to make things right. And now he'd never have the chance.

He felt about a hundred years old as he wiped his hand down his cheek. "How did you end up marrying my brother?"

Chills racked her body as Holly debated Jet's question. The baby snuggled into her side and let out a big yawn. She wished he would go away so she could nap with Clara.

Holly had seen Jet at the funeral—met his eyes, in fact—and had been so stunned at the similarity to Cody's, she'd fled the church and driven all the way back to Cheyenne without a word to him or his family.

What could she say to them? They clearly hadn't known about her, and she certainly hadn't known about them. She and Cody had been married less than a week when his truck crashed into a semitrailer. The police hadn't called her—he hadn't gotten around to listing her as an emergency contact on his phone. So she'd found out two days later, and an online obituary had tipped her off to his funeral up north. It had also mentioned the very much alive family—two parents, two brothers and two sisters—he'd left behind. No mention of a wife in the obituary, though.

Those had been bad times.

"We'd been married for six days when he died." The words came out rusty, as if they, too, knew she didn't speak about Cody to anyone. "He told me he wouldn't be in town for a few days, so I didn't think anything of it when he didn't come home." She began coughing again, each heave like sandpaper grating against her raw lungs.

"Six days?" He mumbled something she

couldn't make out. "We didn't know about you. We would have—" He abruptly stood and paced in front of the chair, rubbing his chin the entire time.

He had the same build as Cody, but he was solid muscle where Cody had been lean and lanky. They shared dark brown hair, too. Jet's was short. Cody had worn his longer. The set of their eyes proved they were brothers. Clara had those eyes. Jet's were full of pain at the moment.

Welcome to the club. Shivers hijacked her body. The past year had gone from catastrophic to rock bottom. Losing Cody had been devastating. Finding out he'd lied to her about not having family hadn't helped. Then, a month later, a positive pregnancy test had turned her life upside down.

Her cousin Morgan had helped her through the birth, but Morgan had moved to Utah soon after, and Holly was doing her best to care for the baby on her own. She'd barely been making it. And two weeks ago, she'd caught her babysitter neglecting Clara. Every time she thought of it, she felt sick to her stomach. Who would harm an innocent baby? Her sweet Clara?

Since then, she'd failed to find a new sitter, gotten fired from her job and had come down with whatever illness she was dealing with now. A respiratory infection, probably. She couldn't afford to see a doctor or pay for medicine at this point. Paying for rent, utilities, formula and diapers were her most pressing concerns.

As soon as she recovered, she was finding a new job, socking away every penny and moving out to Ogden, Utah, to join Morgan. She needed a fresh start, and the pretty town had charmed her when she'd visited once as a child.

"How long did you know Cody?"

"Three weeks." Three weeks that seemed a mirage, a distant dream. "We eloped."

Jet sank back into the chair, still looking like he'd had the shock of his life. "Three weeks. Including the marriage?"

"Yep." She was in no shape to have this conversation. Her bones were the consistency of Silly Putty, and she could barely keep her eyes open. If he wanted to lecture her, fine, but she'd already berated herself enough over her stupid impulse to marry a man she'd barely known.

Wasn't the first time she'd rushed into a romance without thinking. At least she hadn't married the other jerks.

Not that Cody was a jerk. He'd been attentive, exciting.

And a liar.

"Where?" he asked. "Did you get married here? Did you have a reception?"

"Vegas." For two weeks, she and Cody had

spent every minute together when they weren't working. And one night he'd gotten a gleam in his eyes and said they should go to Vegas. Get married. Start their life together now. Who needed a big wedding? The only family she talked to was Morgan, so a big wedding had been out of the question, anyhow.

"And he never mentioned me?" Creases deepened in Jet's forehead. "Or our family?"

She shook her head. He seemed truly hurt. Once she realized Cody had lied to her, she'd assumed it was because he didn't like his family. But the few minutes she'd observed them at the funeral, they'd seemed tight-knit. The whole thing had felt so off, she'd fled from there and done her best to put it out of her mind.

"Why would he do that?" he asked.

"I don't know." If she didn't know better, she'd think he was about to cry. But this guy seemed too tough, too in control, to show that level of emotion. "Look, I don't feel so good. I'm sorry you found out about us like this, but I don't think there's anything more to say."

Just let me be sick in peace.

"Nothing more to say?" His voice rose. "My brother got married, told you he didn't have a family and now I find out he has a daughter, and you think there's nothing more to say? I want answers. I *need* answers."

Why did she feel so hot all of a sudden? Maybe because she wanted answers, too. She needed answers more than he did. *Why, God, did You let this happen? I could have handled Cody pretending he had no family, but I can't handle doing this all alone.*

"He had a life I knew nothing about." Jet dropped his forehead into his hands.

Exactly what she'd thought when she'd read the obituary.

But she did know her husband. He'd grown up on a cattle ranch and shot a rattlesnake about to strike his dog, Buddy. When a girl he went to high school with fell through a frozen reservoir, he'd pounded out a large hole in the ice and personally hauled her up. Gotten sick from it, too. He'd done well in school—valedictorian—and come to Cheyenne because he'd wanted to experience other places.

Cody had been larger than life, a born storyteller, and…secretive. He hadn't allowed her to see his apartment. She didn't even have the address. After the wedding, he'd moved in with her. He'd planned on bringing his stuff over the following weekend.

She fixed her attention on her hands, her wedding ring in particular. She wasn't sure why she still wore it. Truth was, she'd never felt married.

Exhaustion swept her under like the rolling

tide. It was so warm in here. She'd close her eyes…just for a moment.

A cool hand touched her forehead. Her eyelids flashed open. Jet hovered near her.

"You're burning up. Come on. I'm taking you to the urgent care."

"No, I'm fine." She tried to rally, but she had no energy left.

"You're not. You could have pneumonia. Let's go. The sooner you get medicine, the better it will be for Clara."

"Jet—" His name was a plea on her lips, and it felt natural and foreign at the same time.

"Yes?" His voice sounded gravelly.

"I don't have the money…" Shame filled her to her core. No money. No job. No way to protect her daughter.

"Well, I do. And I'm paying." He pointed to the closet. "Your coat and shoes in here?"

"Yes."

"Stay put. I'll get whatever the baby needs if you tell me where to find it."

Within minutes, Clara was bundled up in her car seat, and Holly was sitting in the passenger seat of her car as Jet drove. Her rash decisions and lack of funds had made her and Clara too vulnerable. She had to get her act together. But in the meantime, she'd let Jet take charge. Just this once.

* * *

What had started as an unlikely quest for answers about his brother had turned into a confusing dilemma.

Jet held a takeout cup of coffee in his hotel room the next morning and stared out the window at the snow falling outside. He hadn't planned on spending the night in Cheyenne, but after Holly's bronchitis diagnosis yesterday, he couldn't, in good conscience, leave her and the baby on their own.

Last night he'd called his parents. They'd been as shell-shocked as he was about learning Cody had a wife and child. But their stunned silence had quickly turned into joy. He'd never forget his mom's reverent tone as she'd shakily declared she was a grandma. And Dad hadn't sounded this hopeful since long before they'd found out Cody had died.

Should Jet take their advice and ask Holly to come to Sunrise Bend for a few days? Or should he leave his number with her and go back solo?

The right thing to do was to ask Holly to come back and meet the family. But a part of him didn't want to.

Jet took another sip of the black coffee. He'd been the responsible big brother his entire life. Lately, the responsibilities felt more like burdens. He and Blaine had been trying to figure out the best way to split the ranch between them. They'd done everything in their power to include Dad. At least their father had gotten the legal stuff out of the way. But as for being out on the actual ranch? He showed no interest in it anymore, and it was breaking Jet's heart.

In some ways, he felt like he'd lost his baby brother and his dad in the accident. As the oldest sibling, it was his duty to take on the role of patriarch whether he was equipped for it or not.

Lord, Mom told me You would want me to bring Holly and Clara back to the ranch for a day or two. I know she's right. But my gut tells me they need more, and I don't know if I can handle any more on my plate right now.

As he looked around the hotel room, regret and longing hit him. For years he'd wanted to travel. Get out and visit other areas of the United States. He wanted to see the Grand Canyon, walk around Williamsburg, Virginia, drive through Vermont in the fall, check out all the sites in Washington, DC, relax on the beaches of Florida and stroll the streets of New York City.

He tossed the empty cup in the trash. It wasn't that he wanted a different life. He loved ranching. Sunrise Bend was home. He just wanted to see other places, too. Experience them for himself. But ranching was a 24/7, every-day-of-the-year kind of job.

His family needed him. The cattle needed him. And now Holly and Clara needed him.

He was as tied down as a cowboy could be.

Grabbing his keys, he checked to see if he'd left anything behind, then went out to the hallway. Traveling was nothing more than a fantasy. His parents were right. He'd ask Holly to come back for a few days, and they'd all figure out how to move forward from there.

Two more responsibilities to add to his list.

He wanted to help them, to protect them the way he did his sisters. But he didn't think of Holly like a sister. She was a beautiful woman. She seemed nice.

His brother had found someone beautiful and nice.

A lump formed in his throat. *Cody, I wish you had lived. Holly would have made you happy. I'm sure of it.*

Opting for the staircase instead of the elevator, he went down to the lobby, checked out and strode outside to his truck. There wasn't much wind this morning, thankfully.

He drove out of the lot and, on a whim, decided on a slight detour. What would it hurt to drive past the Wyoming capitol building before returning to Holly's apartment? He might not have another chance to get away from Sunrise Bend anytime soon.

When the grand, imposing structure came into view, he fought the urge to park. What he wouldn't give to go inside and take a tour. Sighing, he drove on, pulling into a drive-through. He had no idea if Holly liked coffee or not, but he would bring her one.

Five minutes later, he stood in front of her door, carrying two coffees and waiting for her to answer his knock. When she opened it, he studied her, noting she appeared to be doing better. Her hair hung over her shoulders in damp waves, and she wore a sweatshirt and joggers. She coughed into her fist before moving aside to let him in.

"Wasn't sure if you wanted one." He handed her the takeout cup. "It's a latte. Has honey in it. Thought it might help your throat." Her slight frown as she accepted it told him she probably wasn't a fan. "You don't have to drink it."

"You got me a latte?"

Those big blue eyes blinked at him. They looked tired. More than tired. Beat down. He waved her to the living room. No sense in making her use up all her energy over something as simple as a latte.

Were those tears welling in her eyes? *Yikes.*

"Thank you. That was thoughtful of you. Very kind."

Thoughtful and *kind* were not the adjectives

people typically used to describe him. *Dependable* and *hardheaded* were more like it.

Clara was buckled into the chair again, and she started bouncing when she saw him. He set his cup on the end table and crouched in front of her. "Hey, you. I'm your uncle Jet."

Her little tongue stuck out as she blew bubbles.

Holly brushed past him, quickly took the baby out of the seat and held her close, the same as yesterday. Strange. She acted like she needed to protect the baby from him or something.

"How are you feeling?" he asked.

"Much better." Her hollow cheeks and the dark smudges under her eyes told a different story, though. "Fever's gone. I think the antibiotics are working. Thank you again. I'll repay you for the doctor and the medicine…"

Holding his hand up, he shook his head. "Nope. It's on me. Don't even think about it."

"But—"

"No buts. Decision's made. It's final." He gave her the look he reserved for his siblings—the one they obeyed. "I talked to my parents last night, and they'd like to meet you."

She turned her attention to the baby. "They would?"

"Yes, my mom has wanted to be a grandma for a long time. You've made her one of the happiest women in Wyoming. Plus, she's worried about you taking care of yourself being sick and all."

"She *wants* to be a grandma?" Holly's forehead wrinkled in disbelief.

"Yeah. Been pestering me and Blaine and our sisters to get married and get on with it for years."

"None of you are married?"

"Erica's engaged. She's getting married in June. The rest of us are single."

"How many of you are there?"

"Five." The truth dropped the bottom out of his stomach. "Make that four. I keep forgetting Cody's gone."

"I'm sorry."

"I am, too."

The baby made a few chirpy sounds, and Holly stood, shifting her to one arm. "Be right back. She needs her bottle." She swayed slightly.

"Here, why don't you let me hold her while you get it?" He rose, holding his arms out.

"No!" She backed up a step. "I do this all the time."

"Do you have a problem with me being near Clara? I won't hurt her."

"No, I just don't know you." She hurried to the kitchen, where she awkwardly held the baby while she made up the bottle. When she returned, she was visibly paler than a few minutes ago.

"Why don't you come to the ranch for a day

or two? Meet my parents. You can rest, recover from your illness. We'll help with the baby. Then I'll drive you back here."

"No, thank you." She pursed her lips and settled Clara into her arms with the bottle.

"Mom loves babies. She's great with them. And you'd have your own room. The ranch is big."

"I can't."

He regarded her as she fed the baby. She looked so tired and resolute and full of love for Clara. His own heart did a somersault. What would it be like to come home to a wife and child? To have someone who would love a baby—his baby— with as much devotion?

He thrust those thoughts from his head. A wife was another responsibility he was not willing to take on at this point in his life. Kids, either. He could barely keep up with everything as it was. It wouldn't be fair to add a wife to the mix. He had no time for one.

"Is it work?" he asked. "Maybe you could call them and get the day off? I don't think you should work being sick and all, anyhow."

Her jaw tightened. "No, I'm between jobs at the moment."

Without a job, how would she afford the rent for this place? Or pay for the baby's needs? This was a hiccup he didn't like.

"You can meet the family—your family now, too—and have a short break."

A coughing fit came over her, making the bottle fly out of her hand. Clara's face puckered and she began to cry. Jet reached over, picked up the bottle and handed it back to Holly.

Their eyes met. Exhaustion and doubts swam in hers.

"We'll respect your wishes regarding Clara." He'd go out on a limb. Maybe she was scared to let anyone near the baby. "If you're not comfortable with any of us holding her, we understand."

After what felt like an eternity, Holly narrowed her eyes. "You mean it?"

"Of course."

"Okay, then. I'll come."

He blew out a soft exhalation. He'd won the battle. But he had a feeling he was on the losing side of a war—a war that would cost him. But what choice did he have? Holly and Clara were family, too. He'd do his best to do right by them. Doing right was all he knew.

Chapter Two

"We're almost there."

Holly wiped the sleep from her eyes in the back seat of Jet's truck as Clara snoozed in her car seat next to her. Checking her phone, she realized she'd slept for almost four hours. She must have drifted off within minutes of hitting the road. Maybe Jet was right. Her body needed the rest.

The truck bumped down a long, gravel road. Gray mountains streaked with white loomed in the distance, and snowcapped trees were scattered on either side of the road.

Nervous tension gripped her muscles. Would Cody's family like her? Jet had said his mom loved babies and wanted to be a grandma, but was it true?

Her own mother certainly didn't. When she'd called her mom for the first time in years to let her know she was pregnant, the conversation had left her charred. *What are you telling me for? You made your bed. You lie in it. I'm not baby-sitting.* As if Holly would ever ask her to baby-sit. The woman had barely taken care of her as a kid. She wouldn't subject her own sweet baby to such terrible treatment.

Holly was on her own. She hadn't seen her father since preschool, and she was officially no longer on speaking terms with her mother. The last person she'd trusted Clara with was Doris, the woman who'd babysat Clara and five other children in her home. Doris had fooled her into thinking she was trustworthy.

Holly should have recognized the signs of neglect. The way Clara gulped down a full bottle every day after Holly's shift as an assistant manager for a bath and body shop. The diaper rashes, the crying jags whenever Holly set her down.

It had taken a couple of weeks of being away from Doris to get little Clara back to the happy, trusting baby she'd been before Holly had returned from maternity leave. And she intended to keep her that way.

The truck slowed as a ranch came into view. Cattle grazed in the pastures. She craned her neck to see everything. Numerous buildings, including a large barn, corrals and stables were visible beyond the sprawling home.

Why would Cody ever turn his back on this? Why had he claimed he had no family?

Maybe coming here was a mistake. What if they'd treated him badly? And here she was—sick, without a car to escape.

Once again, she'd rushed into a decision that could hurt her and the baby.

She'd just have to keep Clara close to her until Jet drove her back to Cheyenne.

He parked the truck and twisted to look back at her. The slight curve of his lips sent flutters to her tummy. Or maybe it was the fact that she'd only eaten a handful of crackers along with the latte and antibiotics all day. Not that she had an appetite. Nothing sounded good, except a soft bed and eighteen hours of uninterrupted sleep.

"You okay?" The concern in his eyes took the edge off her anxiety. She had to admit she felt safe with him.

He'd been kind to her. He was a take-charge type of guy. She'd had several boyfriends, and none of them had his aura of authority.

As long as he respected her wishes with Clara—which he had up to this point—she needn't worry about him.

He got out and opened the door for her. Offered his hand to help her down. Her legs were noodley, and a wave of fatigue hit her along with the cold air.

"Want me to carry the car seat?" He waited for her permission. She nodded, quickly raising the handle and lifting the seat out of the base. He took it from her, cooing at the baby. Another point in his favor.

Clara, clad in a fleece sleeper, yawned, raising her hands over her head. Holly tucked the blanket around her to keep her from getting a chill.

Jet slung Holly's bag over his shoulder as she gathered her purse and diaper bag. Then he took her elbow to steady her as they walked up the path to the house. Her anxiety increased with each step. What would they think? Were they going to bombard her with questions about Cody? What if they resented her?

The door opened and an older couple stood in the doorway. The man looked like a grayer version of Jet. Same build, more wiry and weathered, though. And sad. A person could drown in that much sadness. A lump grew in her throat.

The woman had short, layered brown hair, glasses and large hazel eyes. She wore a blouse with a pale blue sweater and jeans. She had the plump, kind look of a woman happy to be with her family.

"Oh, praise Jesus!" With tears streaming down her cheeks, she wrapped Holly into a hug. "When Jet called last night, I couldn't believe my ears. Our Cody getting married without telling us? It seemed impossible. But then he mentioned the baby and…" She stepped back, clasping both Holly's hands, her eyes shining with so much light it could have blinded a person. "Thank you for agreeing to come. I'm Julie, and this is my husband, Kevin. Welcome to our home."

"Hello," Holly said.

Kevin's brown eyes—the same ones Cody, Jet and Clara had inherited—were bright and watery as he mumbled a greeting.

She stayed close to Jet as they went inside. After taking off her coat, she removed Clara from the car seat.

"Oh!" Julie cried as she covered her mouth. "The baby! She's so precious." She reached her hands out to take her, but Holly backed up a step. Julie's eyes widened briefly, but she recovered quickly and urged everyone to go to the family room.

Jet touched Holly's sleeve. "Are you okay? I know it was a long ride and you're still pretty sick. I can show you to your room if you want to rest."

She wasn't okay. She *was* sick. But the warmth of the Mayers made her want to stick it out for a little while before retreating.

"I'm okay. I'd like to get to know your parents first."

With a concerned expression, he nodded.

"Want some water? A snack? Does Clara need a bottle or anything?"

"Water would be good. I have a bottle ready. If you could run it for a minute under warm water, that would be great."

He led the way to an enormous room with lofted ceilings and large windows revealing views of the distant woods and mountains. A fire crackled in the huge fireplace, and large, comfortable furniture had been arranged around the room.

"I'll be right back with the bottle." He disappeared in the other direction.

"Jet told us you're sick. Why don't you lie down here?" Julie fluffed a pillow and placed it on the end of the couch. Then she unfolded a soft, cream-colored blanket.

Holly was taken aback. She hadn't expected them to actually take care of her. Still holding Clara, she sat on the couch. Julie set the blanket next to her and beamed. Then she went to the love seat opposite. Kevin sat beside her.

An awkward silence fell. A pop from the wood in the fireplace made her jump. Thankfully, Jet returned, handing her the bottle, which she promptly checked to make sure it wasn't too hot. Clara reached for it, and she settled her in her arms and began to feed her.

"This is Clara." Jet pointed to the baby. He

perched on the arm of the oversize chair adjacent to her. "Almost four months old, right?" He looked to her for verification.

"Yes," she said, grateful for the conversation starter. "Clara Lee Mayer. I wanted her to have something of Cody's."

Kevin placed his hand on Julie's knee and she covered it with her own.

"They share a middle name." Julie sounded choked up. "How did you meet?"

"My cousin Morgan was dating one of Cody's coworkers. She had a New Year's Eve party, and we hit it off immediately." He'd met her gaze across the room and glued himself to her side. His laughing eyes had drawn her to him. "He told me a corny joke and…" A stab of pain in her temples cut off the rest of the words.

She'd thought they were meant to be. Love at first sight and all that. And he'd died. Then she'd found out he hadn't been honest with her. That he'd lied—about all of this.

"You loved him," Kevin said quietly.

Unable to speak, she nodded, averting her eyes to avoid the tears.

"I wish we'd known. About the wedding. About all of it." Julie wrung her hands. "Do you have any pictures?"

Holly nodded, swallowing to ease the pain.

"I have pictures on my phone. I'll show them to you later."

"Your parents must have been happy." Julie watched her carefully. "Did your father give you away?"

"I don't have any contact with my dad. Not much with my mom, either. No brothers and sisters. Cody and I eloped."

Julie's face went slack.

"We went to Vegas." Was this going to be an issue? Maybe she wasn't up to talking, after all. Brought up too many memories and invited questions and judging. "Six days later, he died."

"Six days." Julie shook her head. "I'm sorry, Holly. I wish you could have had a long life with our boy. We loved him very much."

Holly believed her, which made her wonder, yet again, why Cody hadn't told her about them.

Kevin made a strangled noise and pointed to her. "Why is she wearing your ring, Jet?"

Jet's ring? Holly straightened, firming her grip on the bottle and the baby.

"What do you mean?" she asked.

Jet's jaw worked as he shook his head at his father.

"Cody proposed to me with it." Holly glanced at Jet, then at Julie and back to Kevin.

"My mother gave Jet the ring before she died." Kevin didn't sound angry, just confused.

"What are you saying?" she asked.

Everyone seemed to be enthralled with the floor all of a sudden.

They didn't have to explain. She figured it out. Cody had stolen the ring from Jet. He'd proposed to her with a stolen ring and lied to her about not having a family.

Had anything about her marriage been real?

A choking sensation gripped her, igniting a coughing spell she thought would never end. When it passed, she slumped, drained and exhausted. "I think I'll take you up on that offer to go to my room, Jet."

His eyes swam with sympathy. "Right this way."

After showing Holly and Clara to a guest room upstairs at the end of the hall, Jet returned to the family room. The past twenty-four hours had been a shock to him and more so for his parents. They hadn't even had a full day to digest this new information. With Holly and Clara upstairs, he'd do his best to fill in the blanks for his parents so the rest of the visit could go smoothly. It would do none of them any good if they scared her off at this point.

He just hoped his brother and sisters didn't barge in and turn the place into a circus. At least

Mom and Dad had convinced them to stay away this long.

"Let's take this elsewhere." Jet gestured for them to follow him. He marched down the hall, through the U-shaped kitchen, to an eat-in area with a long table where they ate most of their meals. He took a seat and waited until they were settled. "We need to get things out in the open before Holly comes back down or we might offend her. I don't want her feeling unwelcome here."

"I don't, either." Mom lifted her steepled fingers to her chin. "I want to be part of our grandbaby's life. Isn't she the most precious thing?" Her eyes filled with tears again as she smiled. "I can't wait to hold her."

"How could Cody do this?" Dad shook his head. "How could he get married and not tell us? And why are we just now learning we have a grandchild?"

This was the tricky part. He'd kept the phone conversation with them short last night, figuring one revelation at a time would be plenty. Unfortunately, he hadn't shared the most painful one. Knowing Cody had disowned them all had cut him to the quick. It would devastate his parents.

God, please give me the right words. Dad has lost so much this year. I don't want this to send him into another downward spiral.

Jet looked at the two people he loved most in the world and steeled himself to break their hearts.

"Cody told Holly he was an orphan. An only child."

Dad blanched. Mom gasped, her hand to her mouth. And Jet ground his teeth together, waiting.

"Why would he do that?" Her horrified expression made him want to go five rounds with the punching bag he and Blaine had set up in the basement during their football days.

"It's my fault." Dad's jaw clenched.

"It wasn't your fault, Dad." Jet was surprised at how calm his voice was. "You gave him more than one warning to get his act together or bear the consequences."

"I was too hard on him." Dad raked his fingers through his thinning gray hair.

"His irresponsibility was hurting the ranch. I was worse to him than you were." And Jet had to live with it the rest of his life. He'd told Cody that if he wanted to waste his life smoking pot and getting drunk, fine, but he needed to do it somewhere else. "We had to put Jaycee down because of him."

Euthanizing the dedicated horse had been one of the worst days of Jet's life. All because Cody had been too impaired to saddle her properly.

He'd ridden her recklessly and gotten tangled in the stirrups. The horse had gone down, breaking her leg in the process.

It had been the final straw for them all. Dad. Him. Even Blaine, who typically stayed out of family drama. Erica had been so upset with Cody, she'd said "Good" when Jet had told her he'd moved out the next day. Their youngest sister, Reagan, had been the only sibling to urge Cody to stay, and she, like Dad, had withdrawn, gotten quiet after his death.

"I'm… I'm just so disappointed." Mom began sobbing softly. Dad patted her shoulder awkwardly.

Jet got up and wrapped her in a hug. This was the hard part for him. He hated that he couldn't take away her pain. His mom was the heart of this family.

After a while, she wiped her eyes and blew her nose. "I didn't get to meet Holly, or help plan the wedding, or throw a baby shower or anything. And worst of all, it makes me miss Cody all over again. I keep seeing that grin of his. Or I'll remember him as a boy, how he'd sneak a cookie and climb onto my lap for a story. And he's gone. Gone."

The sound of the front door opening alerted Jet to a new set of problems.

His siblings had arrived.

Let the games begin.

"Why didn't you call me last night and tell me we have a sister-in-law?" Tossing her purse on a chair, Erica stormed to the table, getting into Jet's face. Her long, wavy, dark brown hair was pulled into a ponytail, and she wore jeans and a cowl-necked royal blue sweater. Slim and tall, she was a force of nature.

"Did Cody really have a baby?" Reagan trailed behind her. Dreamier than Erica, she had light brown hair and a tender heart. "Is it a boy or a girl? I can't wait to hold it!"

Like mother like daughter. Jet didn't bother saying anything because he knew it would be a while before he'd get a word in edgewise anyhow.

"A wife. A kid." Blaine shook his head, dazed. "And he didn't tell us? I always thought I'd be in his wedding. We'd throw him a bachelor party—"

"Yeah, well, I hardly think missing a stag party is our biggest problem here, Blaine." Erica glared at him then turned to Jet. "What's she like?"

"Is she nice?" Reagan crept closer to him. "And the baby—boy or girl? What's its name?"

"Girl," Jet said. "The baby's name is Clara. And Cody's wife's name is Holly. She's nice." Holly seemed genuine. Overprotective, for sure, but she probably had a good reason to be.

"Clara!" Reagan turned to their mother. "Did

you see her? Hold her? Is she cute? Does she look like Cody?"

"Kids." Mom raised her chin and used her you'd-better-listen-up voice. "Sit down. We'll tell you what we know."

Everyone pulled out a chair and did as they were told. Blaine sat next to Jet. Erica and Reagan sat across from them. Mom was at one end. Dad at the other.

"Are the cattle okay?" Jet whispered to Blaine. Blaine gave him a quick nod. He hadn't been gone from the ranch overnight in a long time. A never-ending list of things to check scrolled through his mind. They would have to wait. He had to deal with this family crisis first.

Mom folded her hands on the table and made sure she had everyone's full attention before speaking. "I know this is a shock, but I pray you'll all see this as a blessing. You have a new sister, and you're officially aunts and uncles."

Jet carefully watched his sisters. Erica pursed her lips. Reagan beamed. He didn't need to look at Blaine to know he'd shrugged. Dad still looked a bit peaked. He'd never been all that talkative, and he certainly wasn't now.

"Holly is fighting bronchitis, so I expect you all to be extra gentle with her. It had to be difficult for her to agree to come here. Also, Jet shared some hard news with us." Mom seemed to be choking back her emotions. She met his eyes, and he nodded. It was his cue to take over.

"Cody told Holly he was an orphan." The gasps didn't deter him. "And an only child."

"What?" Blaine shot to his feet. "How could he? Why? What did we do to him? This is—"

"Unacceptable." Erica's cheeks had flushed, but her brown eyes flashed with pain and uncertainty.

"Why would he do that?" Reagan's forehead creased as she met Jet's eyes. He hated to see the sheer devastation in them. "Why would he pretend we don't exist? We all loved him…" She clumsily stood and ran in the direction of the powder room.

Dad stood, too. "I'll see to her."

Jet was surprised. His dad had been like a walking coma patient for the better part of the year. The fact that he was willing to check on Reagan was a step in the right direction.

"Look, I don't know Cody's intentions," Jet said. "But there's nothing we can do about it now. We can't change what happened." No one was making eye contact. Why did the hard stuff always fall on him? *Because I'm strong enough to handle it.* He braced himself. "Holly is upstairs resting with the baby. When she comes down, we need to put our feelings aside and think about her needs."

"What's she like?" Erica asked.

"I don't really know. She seems nice. She was coughing, barely able to stand on her two feet and feverish when I met her yesterday, and she slept all the way here. She's an only child and doesn't have much of a relationship with her parents."

Erica nodded, looking stronger. "So we need to tone it down."

"Yeah." He knew Erica would read between the lines. "She's not used to a big, loud, opinionated family."

"Blaine, you okay?" Mom asked softly.

He'd slumped in his chair. A rush of sympathy came over Jet. The most easygoing of the siblings, Blaine had a lost look about him.

"No, Ma, I'm not okay. I'm never going to be okay with my baby brother cutting me out of his life and pretending I didn't exist." He got to his feet. "I'll meet her later."

"Wait, Blaine," Jet said.

"I've got to check on the pregnant cows." His jerky movements were unlike him, and Jet made a mental note to have a heart-to-heart with his brother soon.

Dad and Reagan came back in. She returned to her seat.

"What did we miss?" Dad's color had returned.

At least Jet didn't have to worry about him falling deeper into his funk right now.

"Nothing. Just that Holly and Clara are family, and we're all going to do our best to make them feel comfortable." Jet turned to each family member and met their eyes. "She's been keeping the baby real close, so I think you should wait to ask to hold her."

Reagan's face fell another notch. "But—"

"Your brother's right. Holly doesn't know us. It might take some time for her to trust us enough to let us be near the baby."

"Well, how long is she staying?" Reagan asked.

"I'm not sure. A day or two." Jet rubbed the back of his neck. Another problem he'd have to deal with. He'd have to take another day off to get her back to Cheyenne.

He was already getting a headache thinking about the next couple of days. Every cow, every bull, every steer mattered to him. While Holly was here, he fully planned to be outside, riding his horse, Rex, to check cattle. His parents and sisters could figure out how to get along with Holly.

But what if they didn't?

Blaine needed his help. But Holly might need his help here, too. A no-win situation. He should be used to it by now, but he wondered if it would ever change. When would he be able to just live his life?

Never. That's when.

Good manners prodded her to go downstairs and talk to the family. Holly lay on her side two hours later, looking down at Clara on the pretty quilt covering her bed. Learning her wedding ring was Jet's had thrown her into a tailspin. But he hadn't made a big deal about it. And, after the nap, she'd found some peace. For the first time in months, a deep sense of relief filled her.

Finally, she didn't have to do all this alone.

But that didn't mean she could let her guard down. Cody's parents had clearly been upset they hadn't been invited to the wedding. She cringed. Did they even know Cody hadn't told her about them?

Clara made babbling noises and grabbed a fistful of Holly's hair.

"Hey there, peaches." Her heart gushed with love for this child. "I know we need to go back downstairs, but don't worry, I won't let anyone hurt you."

What was she going to do if Julie asked to hold Clara again? Her vision blurred as images of her baby wailing in a crib at Doris's came to mind. Her chest tightened, causing her to cough.

At least she no longer felt feverish or as weak as she had last night. All because of Jet.

Her gut told her Julie was nothing like Doris. In fact, if Jet's parents were anything like him, she could spend a couple of days here without hightailing it to Cheyenne. What did she have to hurry back for, anyway? Unpaid bills, no job and no way to get one until she got her childcare situation straightened out.

Shifting to sit, she picked up Clara. Then she found a fresh diaper in the bag, changed her and kissed the top of her head.

"It's time we got to know your grandparents better." A shiver of anxiety coursed down her spine, but she ignored it. She was being dramatic.

The bedroom had an attached bathroom—another luxury she couldn't quite believe—so she found her brush and, carrying Clara, went to the bathroom and stroked her hair until it waved over her shoulders. She looked tired. Not much she could do about it.

After setting the brush on the counter, she grabbed the diaper bag and carried Clara out of the room. The home was rustic, lived-in and enormous. She counted at least six doors down the hallway, and the staircase opened to the large room she'd sat in earlier. A fire still crackled in the fireplace, and the low hum of conversation made her realize more people had arrived. Two women, from the looks of it.

Where was Jet?

Frowning, she descended the steps, clutching the baby. Her favorite Bible passage was etched in her mind. She hadn't been raised as a Christian, but two years ago, she'd attended a local church with a coworker. It turned out her heart had been waiting for the message of hope and grace and mercy. And from then on, one passage replayed in her mind over and over. It was the latter half of Psalm 56:9. *This I know, God is for me.*

She paused on the bottom step. *Lord, I know You are for me. Whatever happens, help me cling to that.*

"Oh, good, you woke up." Julie rose from the couch. "Have a seat. Can I get you something to eat? Something to drink? You must be famished."

"Oh, um, no thanks." She was kind of hungry in a toast-and-hot-tea type of way. She doubted she could choke down more than the basics. She set the diaper bag on the floor in front of the nearest chair and sat, settling Clara on her lap.

"Why don't I fix us all a little snack in case you change your mind?" Julie gave her another warm smile and headed to where Holly assumed was the kitchen.

"Hi, I'm Erica." A striking, tall woman with a blue sweater addressed her. "I was—am—Cody's older sister."

"And I'm Reagan." Another woman, shorter and slim, closer to her own age—maybe younger—sat there, too, looking shy. "Technically, also Cody's older sister. He was the baby. I'm a year older than him."

"I see." She tried to swallow the sudden knot in her throat. "I'm Holly, and this is Clara."

"She's so beautiful." Reagan's flash of dimples lifted her spirits.

"Thanks."

"I'm sorry, Holly." Erica's features oozed compassion. "This must be really hard for you. We didn't know Cody was married, or we would have helped you through all this. I can't imagine what you've been going through."

She believed her.

"Mom told us you were only married for a week." Reagan clapped her hand over her chest, shaking her head. "How horrible. To lose him so suddenly. It was terrible for us, but you must have loved him…"

"I did." But she wondered if it was true. She'd fallen in love with the man Cody presented himself to be, but some of what he'd presented was clearly false.

"Our brother Blaine had to deal with the cattle or he'd be here, too," Reagan said.

"He's freaked out. Jet's out there with him." Erica crossed one leg over the other. "You'll like Blaine when he comes around. He's pretty mellow."

Mellow. Not a description she'd pin on Cody. Or Jet. Cody had been spur-of-the-moment, hyper, volatile. Jet seemed to be strong. Strong-willed. Used to people doing what he said.

"It's been so hard on us all with Cody gone." Reagan's eyelashes dipped.

Erica reached over and covered her sister's hand. "He's in Heaven. We can take comfort in that."

Their response made Holly feel better. Because they'd loved Cody. And if they'd loved him, they might find it in their heart to love his baby, too.

"Here we are." Julie bustled in, holding a tray in both hands. A teapot and china cups clattered, and a plate mounded with baked goods looked ready to topple over. She set it on the coffee table in front of them and began to pour. "Erica, hand this toast to Holly, please."

Was Julie a mind reader? The smell of the toasted bread made Holly's stomach growl. She took a nibble as she kept her grip on Clara, who was getting restless.

"Tea?" Julie held up a cup.

"Yes, please." Holly looked around for the car seat.

"Kevin moved the baby's car seat to the foyer. Reagan, why don't you get it, hon?" Julie finished pouring the tea. "I'd love to take her off your hands, but I understand if you're not ready."

Holly stared down at her sweet girl. Clara had grabbed her feet and was cooing. Then she glanced at Julie, so clearly wanting to hold her grandchild, and fought through the anxiety to do the right thing. At least, she hoped it was the right thing.

"Would you like to hold her?"

Wonder spread over Julie's face and she nodded, blinking away tears. "Yes, please."

Holly stood and brought her over. As soon as she handed the baby to Julie, Clara settled into the woman's capable arms, and Holly realized she had nothing to worry about.

Tears slipped down Julie's cheeks as she held the baby, looking at her as if she'd never witnessed anything so beautiful. "She's the most precious thing I've ever seen. Thank you, Holly. She looks like you, but she looks like Cody, too."

"His eyes."

"Yes." They locked gazes, and understanding flowed between them. They'd both loved Cody. They would both love Clara.

It was that simple.

"Tell us about yourself." Erica settled into her seat, holding her cup of tea, and Holly answered questions about where she grew up and what she did for a living. She asked about their lives, too, being careful not to mention Cody out of respect for them. Reagan was single and working with Julie to expand their candle-making business, and Erica, also working with them, was engaged. The wedding was planned for June. Erica would be moving out of town and no longer able to help with the candle business at that point.

An hour later, when all three of the Mayer women had cuddled Clara and finally passed her back to her, Holly knew she'd been given something she'd never anticipated. A loving extended family for her daughter.

And she had Jet to thank.

Dozens of questions about him raced through her mind. Did he live on the ranch? How old was he? How did he spend his days? Was he married? Seeing anyone?

Of all the inappropriate feelings she'd had over the years, this had to be the worst.

She simply could *not* be attracted to her dead husband's brother.

If there was ever a time she needed to fight her impulsive reactions, this was it. She was a mother now. With responsibilities. It was up to her to protect and raise her baby. And to do it, she needed a clear head.

Jet Mayer was off-limits. In the meantime, she'd push away those questions good and hard.

Chapter Three

Monday afternoon Jet figured it was time to pull Holly aside to find out when she wanted to return to Cheyenne. Yesterday a snowstorm had kept them on the ranch, but the roads were clear now. They'd tiptoed around the subject last night after supper, and he'd been convinced she'd been truthful when she said she'd been enjoying getting to know the family and didn't mind staying a bit longer. Selfishly, he was glad she'd stayed. She and the baby had breathed new life into his parents and his siblings. But he couldn't expect Holly to stick around forever because they'd all been smitten by an adorable infant.

Holly had her own life. One she'd kindly placed on hold for the moment.

He strode through the back door, shucked his coat in the mudroom and found her in the kitchen sitting on a stool, holding the baby and chatting with his mom, who stirred something that smelled delicious on the stove.

"Hey, do you have a minute?" Hands in his pockets, he rocked back on his heels. Flutters in his stomach made him frown. He wasn't one to get nervous. What was his problem?

"Sure." Holly nodded.

"The stew is all set." Mom wiped her hands on a towel. "I'll watch Clara if you two want to get some fresh air."

Holly blinked then smiled. "It would be nice to go outside. Thank you. Her diaper bag has everything in it. I won't be gone long."

"I know what this little munchkin needs, don't you worry." Mom came over, scrunching her nose and smiling at the baby. "Who wants to see her grammy?"

Holly rose and joined him, pausing to glance back at his mom, who was bubbling over with baby talk.

"Trust me. You have nothing to worry about. My mom and babies go together like peanut butter and jelly." He arched his eyebrows. "Want me to show you around the ranch?"

"Sure." She gave a backward glance to his mom and Clara.

"We can stay inside, if you'd rather."

"No, no. I've seen the view from the window. I'd like to get outside for a bit."

"I'll have you back in no time. I promise."

Her lips curved into a grateful grin. "I'm that obvious, huh?"

"I don't blame you. If Clara was my baby, I'd protect her with everything I had." Now why had he said that? Clara wasn't his baby. He didn't even plan on having kids. Or getting married.

"I know."

Surprised, he glanced at her. "You do?"

"Yeah." She stopped in the hall to slip on her boots and put her coat on. "You've got the protective gene."

The compliment warmed him. He wasn't sure how to respond. So he waited for her to finish layering up, then returned to the mudroom. He put on his coat and led her outside.

The sun shining in the blue sky made the snow sparkle. It was so cold, his eyes watered instantly. Was it too chilly for her, considering she was still recovering from bronchitis? As she tipped her face to the sky, she looked young. At peace.

"How old are you?" The words were out before he could stop them.

"Twenty-five. You?"

"Thirty-two." She was a couple years older than Reagan. For some reason, it made him feel old.

"None of your siblings are married."

"Nope. Erica's the only one willing to take the

plunge at this point." Distant moos and the *shush* of their feet on the snow broke up the silence.

"Yeah, she told me." She kept her hands in her pockets. "She's leaving the candle business?"

"Yep." After the wedding, Erica would be moving to a new town and working for her husband's company. She'd no longer be able to run Mayer Canyon Candles day-to-day the way she had been. While his mom was smart and a hard worker, she preferred making the candles over managing the business. Reagan helped with both, but she had a more artistic nature, unlike the practical drive of Erica. He'd have to talk to his mom and Reagan about hiring someone—even part-time—to help. The way the business was growing, they might need to hire more than one employee.

"They showed me some of their candles yesterday. I'm really impressed with what they're doing. Those candles would have sold in a hot minute at the store I managed."

"You managed a store?" He glanced at her again, drawn to her pretty face. All weekend he'd been telling himself to stop staring at her when he came in at night for supper. And all weekend he'd been helpless to stop himself.

"Well, I was technically the assistant manager, but I did all the things a manager would. Inventory, hiring, firing, schedules, sales. I started working there when I was twenty years old."

"What kind of store?"

"Bath and body stuff mostly. Candles, too. All their own brand."

"You mentioned being between jobs," he said. Her voice held pride in her work, so it seemed strange she was no longer employed there. "What happened?"

She didn't answer right away. Then she flicked him a look he didn't know how to interpret. "I found out my babysitter was neglecting Clara. When I couldn't find a new sitter, I missed a few shifts and the manager let me go."

A few choice words flitted through his brain, but he clamped his mouth shut.

"It was a little over two weeks ago and… Well, I got sick, and now I'm here, so I haven't had time to get things settled."

"Someone was neglecting Clara?" Each word could have been chipped off a block of ice. That anyone could hurt the innocent, tiny baby was like an affront to his very being.

The entire time Clara had been there, she'd barely spent a minute not being held. If Mom wasn't baby-talking her, Dad was holding her and telling her he'd get her a pony soon, not that a three-month-old baby had a clue. And his sisters took turns holding her, too. Even Blaine, still struggling with the fact that Cody had disowned them, had cuddled the child. What kind of monster could neglect a baby?

"I should have researched her more. She came recommended." Holly's guilt-ridden expression clued him in to why she'd been so overprotective of the baby at first.

"It's not your fault, Holly. The woman took your money in exchange for caring for the baby. The only one at fault is her, and she should be ashamed. Shouldn't be allowed near a kid ever again if you ask me." The more he thought about it, the angrier he got.

They reached a long line of buildings. She let out a small cough. He should take her back. He'd promised her they wouldn't be out long. "Are you cold?"

"No." She shook her head. Her blue eyes were serene. "What are these buildings?"

"The barn holds equipment and the ranch office, and the stables are behind it." He told her about each structure as they walked past them. Then the row of cabins on either side of the drive appeared.

"Who lives here?" she asked.

"That one's mine." He pointed to the large one on the left. "The one across from it was my grandma's before she died. Technically, hers is a cottage. She never failed to remind me of the fact. No cabin for her. Cottage, cabin—I, personally, never saw the difference."

"Why didn't she live in the main house?"

"She didn't want to. She and Grandpa used to live on the other side of the ranch. After he died, she moved to town, but when her eyes got bad, she couldn't drive anymore. So we brought her out here. Fixed up the cottage the way she wanted it. She loved it. She'd sit on the porch and watch everything happening. You didn't hear it from me, but she was a busybody until the day she died."

Holly laughed, and the sound sprinkled through the air like happy chimes.

Happy chimes? He wasn't out here for fun. As much as he was enjoying this, he'd better get down to business.

"Thank you for agreeing to come here, Holly." He shifted to face her. "Ever since Cody died, it's been tough on everyone, especially my folks. Being able to meet you and spend time with Clara has been good for them. Really good for them. But I told you I'd take you back. I just need you to say when."

Regret flashed through her expression and she sighed. "It's time."

Why did hearing her say it aloud hollow out his chest? He knew the visit had to end. She knew it, too. A gust of wind blew against their faces, causing her to cough. He took her by the arm. "Come on, let's get out of the wind for a minute."

He escorted her to his cabin. It would be home for another year. He was getting ready to build himself a house on his favorite spot on the ranch. Blaine's half of the spread was headquartered several miles away on Grandpa's original site, and Erica and Reagan had both been given twenty-acre parcels of land near the ranch's entrance should they decide to build here, too.

They walked up the porch steps and went inside, halting in the small foyer. Being this close to Holly made him want to get even closer. He could smell her perfume or body spray—something light and feminine and appealing. Her cheeks were pink, and only the slight bags under her eyes revealed she was still fighting off an illness.

There was something soothing about her. Something that made him want to stay in her presence. She made him feel like all the problems he dealt with on a daily basis didn't really matter. And he had no idea why.

"So what's your plan? About the job and all?" He gestured to the couch to the left, and she unzipped her coat and sat. He took a seat in the chair.

"Start putting in my applications." The color

leaked from her cheeks and dejection hung over her like a cloud. "For now."

For now? What did she mean by that?

"My cousin Morgan wants me to move out to Ogden, Utah. She has a little boy. Drake's two. We can help each other out."

Utah? He was taken aback. That was even farther away than Cheyenne. They'd never see her or the baby if she lived there.

"I can't yet, though." She shook her head, her hair rippling over her shoulders like rays of sunlight.

He figured she didn't have the money to move out there. Her apartment had given him the impression she was low on funds, and the lack of job couldn't be helping matters.

"If it's money, we'll help you out." He didn't like her moving out of state, but he certainly wasn't going to let her and the baby fend for themselves. "Do you need a moving van? First month's rent? Some living expenses? We'll take care of it."

The ranch was massive and profitable. It might be full of headaches for him, but money wasn't one of them.

"I couldn't." Her eyes widened in dismay. "It's generous, but I wouldn't feel right. I'll go back to Cheyenne until I can save up enough to move out there."

As they sat with their thoughts, an idea formed. And grew.

It would solve a lot of problems. It would make his family—all of them—happy. And it would benefit Holly and Clara.

But it would cost him.

God, I don't ask for much. My gut tells me this idea is from You. Should I ask Holly to stay?

The urge to blurt it out grew stronger. "Holly?"

"Yes?" She met his gaze. The steadiness in her eyes confirmed he was right to make the offer.

"How would you like to move here for a while? Work with my mom and sisters? The business has been growing so fast, they're struggling to keep up. Erica's barely been able to plan her wedding she's so busy, and Mom and Reagan don't want to deal with the business end."

Her mouth fell open. He wouldn't try to convince her. If she wanted to move here, good. If not, even better. He'd prefer it if she said no.

Because Holly was the first woman in years he was drawn to.

He couldn't deny it. He was hopelessly attracted to his dead brother's widow.

How messed up was that?

Jet was offering her the opportunity of a lifetime, but she couldn't accept it. She had to say no.

It wasn't due to the fact that she'd already

soaked up the goodwill of his family all weekend. Or that Clara was thriving with their abundance of love. It certainly wasn't because they'd given her the physical and emotional support she'd desperately needed ever since finding out Cody had died. They acted like she was one of the family.

No, none of that was the problem. It was her.

This situation felt an awful lot like past relationships she'd rushed into. The only difference? Usually, it was a guy sweeping her off her feet. This was an entire family.

And the worst part? She wanted to be swept off her feet. Needed to have someone accept her. Value her. Love her.

But it never lasted.

She always dove in with off-the-charts expectations and ended up drowning when she found out they didn't need her. The love guys offered seemed like the real deal, but it was fickle. It didn't last.

None of this—the ideal family, the ranch, the acceptance—was meant for her. They might be giving her love now, but they'd show their true colors before long. And she'd be left heartbroken. Again.

"Look, Jet, I appreciate the offer, but I can't." She stared down at the ring on her finger. Jet's grandmother's ring. The one she hadn't returned even though she had to. She knew it. She just hadn't gotten up the nerve. When she did, her time with Cody would officially end—it would be as if the marriage had never happened.

"Why not?" He frowned, and it only made him look more handsome than usual. He was gorgeous enough as it was. Every time he was in the same room as her, she'd find herself peeking his way. It was getting embarrassing at this point. She'd been married to his brother! She had a baby. What was wrong with her?

"I need my own place. It's been wonderful staying with your parents, but—"

"You and Clara can take Grandma's cottage." He tossed it out like it was the simplest solution in the world.

Maybe it was. She could see the cottage's porch out the window from where she sat. It would beat her apartment in Cheyenne, that was for sure, with its loud neighbors, questionable smells and rent she could no longer afford.

"Your mom and sisters might not want me working for them."

He guffawed. "Are you kidding? They'll kiss me for thinking of it. Mom and Reagan love making the candles, but they need business help. And to have you and Clara so close by?" His grin spread, catching her off guard. He brought the word *smoldering* to a whole new level. "Erica's busting at the seams to plan the wedding. And she's not going to be around once it's over."

He was right. Yesterday his sisters and Julie had lamented the fact that the candle business was taking off at the precise moment they needed more help.

"Look, I know this is probably strange for you. Last week you didn't know any of us, and now I'm asking you to move here and completely change your life. I get how it would be unsettling. But we'll pay you a competitive wage. And the position doesn't have to be permanent. It would give you a chance to save up. To move out to Utah like you want."

Up until now, moving to Ogden had felt like an impossible fantasy. If she agreed…she might have enough money to move to Utah by summer.

Hope spread through her chest.

Only to be deflated.

You're doing it again. You're rushing into the dream of it being perfect and all your problems being solved. You, of all people, know it will all crash down sooner rather than later. And you'll be the one who needs them. They won't need you. They already have each other.

Jet crossed his leg to rest his ankle on his knee. "You wouldn't have to worry about finding a babysitter. You could take Clara with you. Between you, Mom, Reagan and Erica, she'll be fine. We could get some baby stuff to put in the showroom where you'd be working."

She could work *and* take care of Clara? She wouldn't have to leave her with a babysitter. No more spending her days frantic with worry that her child was being neglected.

"Think about it. You don't have to give an answer right away."

All her arguments swirled down the drain as she thought of being able to have Clara with her. That alone made it worth it.

She'd have the cottage. She'd have a job. And she'd have Clara with her.

If her fears came true and the family's initial excitement over her and the baby wore off, she'd be okay. A couple of months. That's all she'd need.

She didn't realize she'd been clutching her hands together until she looked down and saw white knuckles.

The ring mocked her.

If she was going to do this, she was doing it right. Quickly, she twisted off the ring and thrust it to Jet.

"Here. This is yours." She met his eyes, darkening like storm clouds. "If you talk to your family and they're okay with me moving into the cottage and working for them, then I accept. But only until I save up enough to move to Utah."

"Fair enough." His words were clipped. "Keep the ring."

She shook her head.

"I mean it," he said. "Cody gave it to you."

"Cody's gone." She pressed the ring into his palm. It was time to let Cody go. Odd circumstances to do it, though. Surrounded by his family. The ones he hadn't told her about.

Life was ludicrous when it came down to it. She'd never understand it. All she knew was that she needed to do what was best for her baby. Living and working on Mayer Canyon Ranch for a few months was the break they both needed.

If she could guard her heart better than she'd done in the past, she'd be okay. If not, she'd muddle through—for Clara's sake.

Chapter Four

Was it even possible to work and take care of Clara at the same time?

She was about to find out. Holly kept a firm grip on the handle of Clara's car seat as she heaved a bulging diaper bag onto her shoulder and locked up. She'd had almost a week to settle into Jet's grandmother's cottage, and she loved it. Vintage and feminine, it suited her and Clara.

Last Tuesday, Jet had driven her back to Cheyenne and helped her pack the apartment. His father had followed them and assisted Jet in loading her car and their two trucks, then the three of them had returned to Sunrise Bend in their separate vehicles. But now it was Monday and time to get used to her new reality. She hoped to learn everything quickly so she could earn her keep at Mayer Canyon Candles.

The icy wind slapped her cheeks as she navigated the frozen path to her car. The pole barn near the main house served as its headquarters and was just over a quarter mile from the cabins. The shortest commute Holly could remember. If she didn't have the baby, she could walk to work.

As she waited for the car to warm up, she took in the glacier landscape and prayed. *Lord, my stomach feels like a volcano is about to erupt in there. I don't know what to expect. Everyone's been so nice to me and Clara. I want to actually help the business, but I don't know if they really need me or just feel sorry for me. Show me how I can be an asset to them.*

Clara made fussy noises from the back seat, so Holly put the car in Reverse and drove down the lane, parking in front of the building. Then she carried Clara and everything else inside.

The first thing she noticed was the smell—a medley of vanilla, cinnamon, oranges and flowers. Then she took in the space. Laminate mimicking hardwood covered the floors. The walls were painted taupe. A kitchen area took up the far left corner. Attractive wooden shelves lined sections of the wall on either side of the room. Two desks faced each other in the far right corner and straight ahead, on the opposite wall, was a door marked Workshop.

The warmth seemed to embrace her as she set down the car seat and took off her coat. Then she lifted Clara out and carried her to the workshop door where muffled voices could be heard.

"I don't know how you can find anything in here. I've told you we need to organize this. It will save time." Erica's strong voice rang clear.

"It *is* organized. I know where everything is." Reagan's softer voice grew louder.

"Will you girls hush?" Julie said. "I'm measuring the fragrance oil."

They'd told her to arrive at nine and she was five minutes early. When did they start working?

She cracked open the door and peeked inside. "Hello?"

Three faces turned her way. All three broke into smiles.

"You made it!" Julie rose from a stool and pushed her glasses up on the bridge of her nose. "And here's our little pumpkin."

Erica strode to her. "Come on. I'll give you the tour."

"Let me finish up this batch and I'll join you," Julie said, taking a seat once more. "Reagan, did you add the dye?"

"I will right now." Reagan stooped, pulling two bottles off a shelf below some sort of workstation.

Holly gave the room a cursory glance while questions ran through her mind. The room had floor-to-ceiling industrial shelving full of supplies along one wall. Straight ahead was a well-lit workstation. The other wall contained a series of workstations with shelving above and below the counters.

"Come on." Erica brushed past her out the door. "We'll start out here."

She followed her. As Clara took everything in with her big brown eyes, Holly couldn't resist kissing the top of her head.

"We set up the desks there, but honestly, I'm the only one who uses this area." Erica rapped her knuckles on one of the desks then gestured to the kitchen area. "When Mom had this barn refurbished, she thought she and Reagan would make the candles in the kitchen, but as the company grew, they set up the workshop in the back."

"Why?" The kitchen looked inviting with its light cabinets and marble-like counter. A coffee maker was half full, and the sight of it made her mouth water. A sink, refrigerator, microwave and small stove made it completely functional.

"Mom never realized standing all day at a kitchen counter would be so hard on her back and knees. Did you notice the workbenches in the back room?" Erica leaned against the counter. "Dad ordered everything to be comfortable with good lighting. The workshop makes their lives easier. All the supplies are at Mom's and Reagan's fingertips, and they can make more products with more stations."

"Ah. Good to know." She'd been selling candles, lotions and such for years, but this was the first time she had a firsthand look at how they were made. "Do you make the candles, too? You mentioned working out here."

"I spend most of my time at this desk. I print the online orders, take care of the income and expenses, order supplies and get everything shipped, in addition to other things that crop up."

With Julie and Reagan making the candles and Erica doing everything else until June, why would they need her?

"You're doing us a big favor, Holly." Erica's clear brown eyes met hers. "I've been worried about what will happen when I get married and move. And, honestly, Jamie's been hounding me to quit and help him run his new dealership."

"Dealership?" she asked. "Like cars?"

"All-terrain vehicles and snowmobiles. He owns three dealerships. He wants my help, and he's been perfectly clear he wants it now."

"Okay, so tell me what to do." Some of her nerves fled at the realization they did need her. This wasn't a pity hire. Well, not solely a pity hire.

Erica laughed. "I like your attitude. Let me finish the tour and we can go over everything."

They made their way around the room. "This is basically our showroom. We bring in tables for displays a couple times a year. We had an open house before Christmas."

Holly paused in front of one of the wooden display shelves to inspect the candles. The labels weren't as eye-catching as she'd hoped they would be. But the scents were sure to be a hit.

"Bathroom's over there. There's an all-purpose room with cleaning supplies across from it." Erica pointed to a hallway then stopped. "Do you mind if I hold her? It's been days since I've had little Clara in my arms."

"Of course." These women loved her baby. The previous months of being alone, in over her head, unable to trust anyone triggered an overwhelming sense of sadness inside her. If she had known Cody's family was this wonderful, she wouldn't have had to go through all that.

What had happened to cause the rift between him and his family?

"Erica, can I ask you a question?"

"Go ahead." She beamed at Clara then gave Holly a curious glance.

"It's about Cody. Why do you think he didn't tell me about you all?"

Erica's face fell and she sighed. "He was mad at us."

"For what?"

"He had some problems, and they became our problems, and he wouldn't listen to us. And when we tried to reach out, he wouldn't take our calls. I don't think any of us saw or spoke to him in the six months before he died."

It answered some of her questions, but it raised more. Like what sort of problems?

Reagan opened the workshop door. "Want me to show you around back here?"

Holly nodded, and Erica hitched her chin to her. "I'll watch Clara while they show you the workshop. I don't think it's safe in there for a baby."

Holly followed Reagan.

"As you can see, most of the room is storage." Reagan's cheeks flushed. "It's kind of messy. Erica thinks we should have a better system." From her tone, she didn't agree. "But the fragrance oils are on this rack, and the dyes are over there. I keep some at the other stations, too."

Holly made a mental note of where everything was kept. It would help her if she had to start ordering supplies.

"And our wax melters and scales are lined up over here. I do a lot of testing at this station." Reagan explained the process of choosing the wax, melting it to a precise temperature and adding dye if the candles were to be colored. At a certain temperature, depending on the scent, the fragrance was also added. "It has to be exact. There's a lot of math involved. Mom and I used to wing it, but now we measure everything carefully. We keep notes on every batch."

"We couldn't replicate our results until we stuck to our formulas." Julie stood, arching her back to stretch it out. "Did you show her our packaging station?"

They moved toward the door where a pegboard held packing tape, boxes, a postage scale and rolls and rolls of labels. Reagan tidied the materials on the counter below the pegboard. "I want customers to open the box and experience Mayer Canyon Candles. So I came up with a packaging technique. The only drawback is that it's time-consuming."

"What an interesting thought—experiencing Mayer Canyon Candles." Holly liked the concept. An experience.

"That's what I thought," Reagan said. "It goes beyond just buying a candle and makes the customer want to buy them again and again."

"Well, girls, I am more than ready for some coffee." Julie opened the door and waited for them to exit before heading to the showroom kitchen. "Reagan, remind me what's on our list for the day."

Reagan took four mugs out of a cupboard.

"Here, I'll help. Do you all take cream? Sugar?"

Holly opened the fridge as Erica brought Clara over and sat on a stool with the baby on her lap.

"Both." All three Mayer women chimed in unison. Then they looked at each other and laughed. Holly poured cream into the mugs, and Julie filled them with coffee. A sugar bowl sat on the counter.

Reagan pulled a folded piece of paper from her pocket and began reading the various candles and melts they needed to make.

"I printed out the order list, you know." Erica glared at the paper in Reagan's hand.

"It's easier for me to remember this way." Once again, Reagan flushed, shoving the paper back in her pocket.

"On scrap paper in your pocket?" Erica shook her head. "What if you lose it?"

"I won't." Reagan blinked.

"You might as well see it yourself on day one." Erica turned to Holly. "They have their own way of doing things."

"Your way isn't the only way," Reagan muttered.

"Girls, we're all given different gifts from the Good Lord." Julie took Clara from Erica, holding her high and scrunching her nose at her.

"Jet mentioned the business has been growing," Holly said. "What are your biggest challenges right now?"

Erica opened her mouth to speak, but Reagan beat her to it. "We need to make more candles every day. We're swamped."

"You need a goal-oriented approach to sales, not the sprinkle-dust method where you're throwing the candles into the wind, hoping someone buys them." Erica sipped her coffee. "At least the Etsy shop took off."

"It did. That was smart thinking, Erica, and the local sales have been increasing, too." Julie shifted Clara to her hip.

"Do you sell the candles in stores?" Holly asked.

"Oh, yes." Julie nodded as Clara rubbed her eyes. "Several stores in town carry them, but most of our orders are through the internet."

"What about stores in other towns?"

"No." Reagan tilted her head and shrugged.

Clara began to fuss. "Let me get the baby carrier. I'll be right back." Holly went over to the diaper bag and pulled out a cloth baby carrier. Soon Clara was strapped to her body, her face looking out to the world and her little legs kicking. "So what can I do to make life easier for all of you?"

"Well, I need to start helping Jamie as soon as possible." Erica placed her mug on the counter. "So obviously someone will have to take over my duties."

"Not me." Reagan visibly shuddered.

"I can take them over, Erica. That's where my experience is anyhow." Holly turned to Julie and Reagan. "Is there anything I can do to free you up to focus only on the candles?"

Neither spoke for a moment as they exchanged a long glance. Then Reagan nodded. "Packaging. No one loves boxing up the orders."

"I would have done it if you'd let me." Erica's singsong voice held a tinge of *I told you so*.

"Honey, packaging everything just right is not your strong suit." Julie patted Erica's hand. "We want our customers to open the box to beauty, not a mess."

"My boxes were not a mess."

"I showed you our technique," Reagan said over the rim of her mug.

"What's the big deal? I wrapped them up in the craft paper and shipped them out." Erica's jaw jutted.

"It's not enough to slap them in some craft paper and—"

Before a war erupted, Holly addressed Reagan, "If you'll show me how you want things packaged, I'll do my best to help you."

"That would be great." Her shoulders visibly softened as relief spread across her face. "Then Mom and I could fill the orders, and I'd have more time to test the new scents."

"We'll move the packaging station near your

desk. That way, you can do it out here with the baby." Julie set her empty mug in the sink. "Well, as much as I'd love to extend this break, we have too many candles to make to stand around. Let's get back at it."

"Come on, I'll show you the ropes." Erica touched Holly's forearm. "Let me grab a chair for you."

Soon Erica was clicking through invoices, expense sheets, suppliers, order forms and too many other things to count. She kept up a steady stream of instructions as she went through it all. Holly took detailed notes, but her head began to swim, and when Clara got cranky, she was glad to take a break to feed the baby.

"When are you planning on quitting here? You mentioned working at Jamie's dealership?" Holly hoped she'd say in a month.

"I haven't told everyone yet, but I'm supposed to start working from home for him next Monday. He wanted me to start this Wednesday, but I told him no way."

One week. One week to cram an entire business into her head.

What if she got it wrong? Messed it all up?

"Don't worry." Erica leaned in. "I'll be right here if you have any questions. We'll basically be working together for a while."

Relief seeped through her bones. For over a

year, she'd gone from one challenge to another. She could do this. She'd make it work. Even if it took her a little while to get the hang of everything.

Jet kept his eyes alert for problems as he and Blaine rode out to check cattle. Today was Holly's first day working with his mom and sisters. Was she doing okay? He hoped they weren't expecting too much of her. Moving to a new town, being surrounded by his big family and recovering from bronchitis had to have taken a toll. Last week he'd done his best to make the move go smoothly, enlisting Blaine and Dad to move her belongings into the cottage, which Mom and his sisters had thoroughly cleaned first. And Mom had insisted Holly take the rest of the week off to get settled.

"I think we need to add another section of corrals at Grandpa's place before I move," Blaine said.

All morning Jet had been ignoring Blaine's comments about moving. His brother was setting up a cattle operation on the old ranch, the part Grandpa ran when Dad was a boy. It was the only logical way to divide it, but Blaine didn't know what he was getting into. Dad had moved all the equipment and horses from Grandpa's ranch fifteen years ago. The place was empty and the outbuildings were all standing, but repairs would need to be made.

"I guess we'll have to share the tractor until I can buy a new one." Blaine's breath spiraled in the cold air. "If we split the herd this summer, we should keep some of the heifers we'd normally sell."

Jet tightened his jaw. Splitting the ranch, dividing the herd and having Blaine move into Grandpa's house five miles away was going to seriously affect everything. He wasn't ready for it, and Blaine certainly wasn't, either. If it wasn't for Dad insisting it was high time the two of them separate and use the land that had been sitting idle, Jet would happily leave everything as it was. Why fix something that wasn't broken?

"Let's get through the calving season and figure it out then." Jet prodded Rex to pick up the pace toward a group of cattle grazing in the distance.

"You've been putting this off for months." Blaine's tone hardened as his horse kept up with Jet's. "I want my own place. You do, too. We have land I could put to good use the way Grandpa and Dad wanted. I don't get why you're dragging your feet."

Jet couldn't deny he was dragging his feet. But a part of him was also ready for the next step. He wanted to build a home of his own. He had the spot picked out and already knew how he'd situate it with views of the mountains and creek. The only thing he didn't have was a house plan.

Who knew when he'd have time to build it? With his sister getting married, Blaine harping on him about splitting the ranch, the candle business growing and Dad still way too withdrawn, Jet couldn't indulge in house plans at this point.

Too many other things were calling for his attention.

Once again, he hoped Holly was getting on okay at the candle shop.

"Look, the pregnant cows are my number one priority," Jet said. "The calves provide our income. I can't afford to get distracted by things that can wait."

"They can't wait, though, Jet. Not forever. I'll be thirty soon."

"Yeah, and I'm thirty-two. So what?"

"So, you're not the one who's stuck taking orders from his big brother every day. I'm ready to be my own boss."

"We're a team." Jet straightened in the saddle. "I don't give you orders."

"You've been giving me and everyone else in this family orders since the day I was born."

Yeah, because he had to keep his siblings in line. It was part of his job as the oldest.

Jet pulled up on the reins and turned to face Blaine. "Do you have a problem with me?"

Blaine sighed. "No. But I'm starting to think you don't want the ranch split. You want it all for yourself."

He wanted to shout he didn't want any of it. It all came with too much responsibility. If Blaine wanted to be in charge, he could go right ahead. He could have it all. For good. Then Jet would pack a bag and board a plane. Go somewhere else for a change. Have a sliver of freedom for once in his life.

Blaine's face was red from the cold, but his eyes had iced over from anger. Or hurt. Jet wasn't entirely sure which. His brother wasn't one to complain or to raise his voice. In fact, a lot of the time, Jet had no idea what went on in his head.

"What's going on with you?" Jet asked. "You're awfully ornery today."

"I'm tired of being in limbo. And Holly being here reminds me life is short."

Holly? Jet sucked in a breath. Was Blaine getting close to her? Jet hadn't seen them together or anything. And he would have noticed if Blaine had stopped by her cabin. His front window faced her porch. He and Blaine worked on the ranch all morning and afternoon. In the evenings, he knew she stayed tucked inside.

This possessive feeling creeping through him

wasn't good. He had no say over Holly's personal life. No claim on her.

"You been spending time with Holly or something?" Jet asked as innocently as possible.

"Me? No." Blaine grimaced. "Don't plan on it, either."

Something light and cheery, like wildflowers poking up in the spring, spread through his chest. Man, he was losing it.

"You don't like her?" he asked.

"Oh, she's nice enough. But when I see her, I think of Cody. It's too hard to be around her for long."

Yeah, there was that. If only he could have the same reaction. When he saw Holly, he saw long blond hair and kind blue eyes and a loving mother and…he wanted to be around her even more.

"You all right?" Blaine asked.

"Why?" Heat rushed up his neck.

"You had a weird look on your face."

"Probably the shredded beef Dad made last night," he said gruffly. "Come on. Let's finish up so we can get out of the cold."

Maybe Blaine was right about splitting the ranch soon and having their own lives, their own ranches. They'd still help each other out. But thinking about everything that would need to be done to make it happen gave him a headache.

Or maybe it was the nagging worry about how Holly was doing.

He could stop by her cabin later. Find out how her day had gone.

Checking on her to make sure she was okay was the right thing to do.

As his heartbeat hammered, he knew it was a lie. He wanted to see her. And this was his excuse to do it.

Today had been exactly what she'd needed. Holly stretched her legs out on the sofa, rested the back of her head on a throw pillow, closed her eyes and let out a deep breath. Her first day on the new job. Fun coworkers. A comfortable environment. And best of all, her baby safe and within reach at all times.

That being said, there were some challenges she hadn't been prepared for. The dynamics of a mom and two sisters running a business had left her a tad exhausted. She wasn't used to people saying whatever was on their minds. She also wasn't used to them bickering one moment and acting like best friends the next.

She'd never had siblings, though. Was it normal? She'd ask Jet about it next time she saw him.

She hoped she'd see him soon. She relaxed as his face came to mind. Ever since she'd moved into the cottage last week, he'd found ways to make life easy for her. Like when he'd picked her and Clara up to eat supper with the family most nights. Or how he'd texted her early this morning to let her know where to park at the workshop so she wouldn't have to figure it out on her own.

And this cottage—oh, it was perfect. Cozy. It had two bedrooms, a surprisingly roomy living area and a small kitchen with attached eating nook. Jet had told her to move things around and decorate it how she wanted. With the exception of a few pictures she'd hung, she'd left it as it was.

As her mind settled, Erica's explanation of why Cody hadn't told her about them lingered. She'd mentioned he'd had problems, which had become their problems. And no one seeing or speaking to him…for how long? Six months? Cody had told her he'd moved to Cheyenne the summer before they'd met. The timing added up.

A knock on the door made her jump. She got up and crossed over to open it. Jet stood on the welcome mat. His lopsided grin made her tummy flip.

"Can I come in?"

She nodded, moving aside for him to enter. Something about his chiseled jaw and probing gaze knocked the words right out of her. Why was he so attractive?

And why was she noticing him—her dead husband's brother—in that way?

"How'd it go today?" He took off his cowboy hat and coat and hung them on a hook on the wall.

"Really good." She gestured for him to join her in the living room. He sat on the chair and she took a seat on the couch, folding one leg under her.

"That's great to hear." His face brightened. Had he been worried about her? "Did they work you too hard?"

She chuckled. "No. I mean, I'm tired, but mostly because there's a lot to learn."

"Is there?" He frowned. "Like what?"

She explained Erica's management system. Reagan hadn't had time to show her the packaging process, so she had that to look forward to at some point. Taking care of Clara had kept her on her toes but hadn't been difficult, probably because the baby had taken an afternoon nap.

"I didn't realize your sister was quitting before the wedding."

"She mentioned it, but I guess I didn't think she would." His eyebrows drew together as he rubbed the back of his neck. "What about the candles? Are you going to make those, too?"

"Oh, no." She shook her head, thankful Julie and Reagan were on top of it. "I had no idea how precise it all is. They measure everything to an exact weight and have to watch the temperature closely. It's quite a process."

"Well, it's probably a good thing they've got the candles covered, what with the baby and all. I can't imagine it wouldn't be safe to have Clara around hot equipment."

"Right." She nodded. "The setup is actually ideal. I can keep her in the showroom with me while they make the candles. And Erica is going to be working in there even when she starts helping Jamie next week, so it should be fine."

"Next week already? She really wasn't kidding." His eyes shimmered with appreciation, and it boosted her confidence. He snapped his fingers. "You'll need a laptop. And stuff for the baby."

"Oh, I'll figure something out." She didn't have the money to buy a laptop or baby gear.

"No, I said I'd take care of it. What kind of things will Clara need?"

Holly considered it. "She's almost to the age where she could use one of those Exersaucers. I already have a play mat and toys I could bring over."

"But then you'd have to bring them every day."

True.

"Don't worry, we'll get you set up. Just send me a list." He hitched his chin toward her. "How did you get on with my sisters? They're best friends, but you wouldn't know it from the way they fight."

"I wouldn't call it fighting…" She aimed for tact, although they'd argued off and on all day.

"I would. They're opposites. It's a good thing you'll be there. Keep them on their toes."

"I like them both very much." It was true. She liked his entire family, even Blaine, who'd said all of three words to her since they'd met. "Is that how it is with you and your brother? You work together, too. Do you argue a lot?"

A pained expression flitted across his face. "No. We get along well. I mean we have our moments. Like today."

She couldn't help thinking about Cody. Had he gotten along with Jet and Blaine? What problems had he caused? Should she ask Jet about it? Erica had given her few details, and Holly needed more. It didn't seem to be the right time, though.

"What happened today?" she asked.

He sighed, shrugging. "We're getting ready to split the ranch, and we don't see eye to eye on everything."

"Split the ranch?" She had no idea what that meant.

"Yeah. Dad's heart isn't into running it anymore. He gave all four of us the option of being involved in the day-to-day operations, but Erica and Reagan declined. Reagan loves the candles, and Erica wants to work with Jamie. So Blaine and I are splitting it and paying our sisters a percentage of the profits. It's the fairest way."

She was impressed they all had a say and a portion of the profits. "How will it work? Do you share the stables and machinery? Who gets the house? Do you eenie-meenie-miney-mo the cows?"

He chuckled. "No, we don't eenie-meenie-miney-mo the cows. My grandpa owned the original ranch. It's five miles from here, connected to our land. He gave Dad a big chunk of property when he was in his twenties. Dad bought up the surrounding land as it became available. When Grandpa died, Dad merged the herds and kept everything here. Blaine plans to move into Grandpa's old house and take half the herd with him."

"And you don't want him to?"

"I want him to. I don't know if he's ready. We have a lot to figure out before we jump into it."

"Like what?" She settled into the couch and watched him. He wasn't an expressive person. Yet his eyes told her everything she needed to know. He was cautious by nature. He didn't want his brother or the ranch hurt by a rash decision on either of their parts.

"Like, if the outbuildings need to be repaired over there or if he'll need equipment. Who he can hire to assist him in daily chores."

"You'll miss him, won't you?" She angled her head sympathetically.

"Me? Nah." He averted his eyes, waving dismissively. "I'll see him all the time. We'll still help each other out."

"It won't be the same, though." She knew it all too well. It was hard moving forward when someone you loved was no longer around the way you were used to them being. She'd had to trudge ahead solo too many times to count. Even her current circumstances were the result of having to move forward without Cody.

"No, it won't."

"So Erica's getting married, Reagan and your mom's business is expanding, and Blaine is moving to the other part of the ranch." Holly studied him. "What will you do with yourself?"

"Me?" He let out a sarcastic laugh. "Same old, same old."

"No dreams to pursue?"

"Nothing special." He caught her gaze. "I'll build a house. Take some trips. It'll be good."

"Building a house, huh?" She enjoyed watching him. He actually looked sheepish for once.

"Yeah. I'll take you over to where I plan on building when it's nicer out. It's here on the ranch."

"I'd like that." She would, too. "Where will you go when you travel?"

"Oh, anywhere."

"That's how Morgan and I always were. We'd sit on her couch and talk about driving to Denver or California. Just getting away and having fun."

"Morgan's your cousin, right? The one in Utah?"

"Yeah. She's kind of bummed I moved here, but she understands I need to save up before I can join her in Ogden."

A shadow passed over his face. She wanted to chase those shadows away. "You must have some destination in mind if you want to travel."

"I'd like to see more of America. I'd take a day trip to Yellowstone at this point. It's been years since I've been out that way. Always wanted to hike around Mammoth Hot Springs."

"I've never been to Yellowstone. Tell me about it."

Jet described the geysers and wildlife he'd seen. She enjoyed watching his animated face. It was obvious he loved it.

"Yellowstone can't be too far from here," she said. "You should go visit when the weather's nicer."

His face fell. "I'll be too busy…" He shifted to stand. "Well, I won't keep you. Let me know what you need for Clara at work, okay?"

"I will." She wouldn't, though. He'd already

done so much. She couldn't take advantage of his generosity.

All the questions she'd been hesitating to ask him about Cody would have to stay there for a while. She wasn't sure she could handle the answers right now, anyway. Why bring up the past when everything was going fine? It would only stir up trouble.

Chapter Five

Friday morning Holly was bursting with ideas to market the candles. With Clara on her hip and two bulging totes full of baby necessities slung over her opposite shoulder, she clumsily opened the door and hurried inside the showroom.

The rumble of the coffee maker and the showroom lights brought cheer to a dreary day. Strangely enough, she didn't detect voices. Usually, muted chatter from the workshop greeted her when she arrived. Where was everyone?

After setting everything near her desk, she took a moment to get her bearings. Jet had stopped by every night this week to see how she was doing, and each night they ended up chatting about their days. It added a dimension to living here she hadn't anticipated. Jet was becoming a friend.

And Reagan and Erica were, too.

She carried Clara to the workshop where Reagan was testing new products. Her concentration was palpable as she poured wax into tea-light containers. The smell was homey. Holly couldn't put her finger on what it smelled like, though.

"Oh, hi, Holly." Reagan set the pitcher down. "And sweet Clara bear. I'm trying a new tea-light blend. I'm calling it Comfy Pajamas."

"That's it." Holly nodded with enthusiasm. "I wasn't sure what I was smelling, but cozy pajamas sums it up."

"You like it then?" Reagan's nose wrinkled as if unsure of herself.

"I love it. And so will our customers." She cringed as she realized she'd inserted herself into the equation. This wasn't *our* business. It was theirs—the Mayer women's.

"Oh, good." She blew out a breath in relief. "I try new scent combinations, but I don't always get it right."

"Nobody gets it right all the time. But this? It's right."

"I'm ready for a cup of coffee." Reagan finished filling the tea lights. "Join me?"

"I was thinking the same thing."

As they headed to the kitchen, Holly could picture a cute label with an illustration of a woman sipping a hot beverage in her pajamas. "Reagan, how firm are you on your current candle labels?"

She looked back at Holly as she poured two mugs of coffee. "I haven't thought about it. Mom and Erica and I had to come up with a design in a hurry, and our current labels are the only one we all agreed on."

Holly wasn't surprised. The labels weren't bad. They just lacked that extra something. "I have an idea for your Comfy Pajamas label."

The door opened to feminine laughter. Erica and a slender, pretty brunette appeared, chuckling about something.

"Oh, good, you're here." Erica beamed at Holly. "I invited Tess over to show her our income and expense reports. She has her own bookkeeping business. Tess Malone, this is Holly Mayer, Cody's wife—er, widow. Holly, this is Tess."

Her stomach hollowed out. Why was Erica bringing in a bookkeeper? Wasn't that part of her duties? Did they think she couldn't handle it?

Could she handle it?

She'd be the first to admit invoicing, ordering supplies and packaging the candles took up most of her day, but she still managed to cram marketing in here and there.

"It's nice to meet you." Tess strode forward, taking her hand and giving it a firm shake. "And who is this cutie-pie?" She pointed to Clara.

"This is Clara, my daughter."

"Look at those cheeks and those pudgy baby fingers." Tess's eyes sparkled as she pretended to be in agony. "It's been ages since Tucker was this little. I miss holding a baby so much."

Holly swallowed. Tess clearly loved babies, and it wasn't like she would snatch Clara and run. But something held her back from offering to let her hold her.

"Let's hope Sawyer puts a ring on it so you can give Tuck a sibling." Erica slung her arm around Tess's shoulders.

"I'm ready for that ring, girl." Tess grinned back at Erica.

"How's your dad?" Erica asked.

"Compared to before Christmas, his rebound has been remarkable. I don't know how long it will last, but it's really nice seeing him doing so well." Tess turned to Holly. "Lung cancer."

"I'm sorry."

"He has a lot of people praying for him," Erica said.

Reagan popped out from behind the kitchen counter and came over to give Tess a hug, which she heartily returned. They caught up for a few moments, leaving Holly in the background and on edge.

"Tess, come smell my new tea lights." Reagan led Tess back to the workshop.

Holly pulled Erica aside. "I thought you wanted me to take over your duties."

"I do." Erica's frown creased the bridge of her nose. "But if you're taking on packaging, you'll be too busy to take care of the books, too."

"I can do some of it." She sounded defensive, but why shouldn't she be? "I was an assistant manager for years. I know what running a business involves."

"I know you do." Erica stepped back. "I didn't mean to offend you. We just need more help. We've needed it for a while."

Maybe Erica was right.

Erica met her gaze. "I want to free you up to do what you do best. It's obvious you pick up on marketing way faster than Mom and I do. Plus, I've heard you on the phone with suppliers. You're a natural at dealing with them and getting the best price."

Hearing Erica's praise wiped away some of her insecurity.

"Mayer Canyon Candles needs more than someone running the numbers." Erica pulled her shoulders back, a visionary gleam in her eye. "It's expanding and could expand even more. I think you're the one who could help get it there."

"I know my way around social media, making graphics, running ads and maintaining a website. I had to learn a lot of it the hard way."

"Me, too." Erica's tone was dry as toast. "You sound like you actually enjoy it, though."

"I do, and I want to earn my keep. If you need me to do the books, too, I will."

"Holly, we need more than one person. You will more than earn your keep. If you want the books, be my guest, but then we'll have to hire someone to help with marketing. Mom and Reagan won't do it. And you won't have time."

She thought about it for a moment. Erica was right. But it would have been nice to have been prepared before Tess came on board. "Okay. I think you're right. But next time, can we have this conversation before you bring in a third party?"

Erica blushed. "Of course. I'm sorry. I didn't think. I'm trying to do everything I can to make sure this place is running smoothly before I'm gone for good."

"I understand." Holly nodded. "You're leaving very hard shoes to fill."

"What a nice thing to say." Erica beamed at her. "Come on. Let's grab Tess and figure out who's doing what."

Friday afternoon Jet parked his truck in front of the candle shop and loped to the truck bed where he'd loaded the boxes. All the office equipment and baby gear had arrived, and he was stacking it inside so he and Blaine could organize it tomorrow. Holly had given him a list of three things for the baby, which he knew couldn't be right, so he'd talked to Mom and gotten the real list. It couldn't be easy on Holly working all day *and* caring for Clara. She'd need a lot more stuff than she'd let on.

If he had his way, she wouldn't feel obligated to work at all, but he wasn't stupid enough to suggest it. She didn't like charity, that was obvious, but she didn't understand this wasn't charity. This was family. His family. And they all looked out for one another. They all did their part, whether helping on the ranch, pitching in with the candle business or supporting each other in general.

They all wanted Clara to thrive.

He hauled a large, long box out of the truck bed and hefted it on his shoulder. Then he opened the showroom door and carried it inside where five pairs of female eyes landed on him.

Oh, boy. What had he walked into?

"Jet! What are you doing here?" Mom bustled over, pushing her glasses up her nose. "What is that? Oh…" She gave him a conspiratorial wink. "The goodies arrived."

"Whatcha got there, big brother?" Erica approached. He recognized the gleam in her eyes. It sent a shiver down his spine. She was too smart for her own good, and he had no doubt she was going to make him squirm. She had a long history of embarrassing him when a group of women was around.

"Baby stuff," he said gruffly. Then he looked beyond her, nodded to Reagan, locked eyes with Holly for two beats too long and realized Tess had joined them. "Hey, Tess. Sawyer hasn't had any calves yet, has he?"

"Hello to you, too, Jet." She rolled her eyes and chuckled. "No, he's waiting on pins and needles, though."

Sawyer was one of his best friends from high school and had recently returned to Sunrise Bend and promptly fallen in love with Tess. Seeing her here reminded Jet he hadn't seen the guys in a while. He should set up a get-together with his buddies. Blaine could probably use it, too. He'd call them all later.

The Watkins brothers, Austin and Randy, had a ranch outside town. Austin was his age. He worked the ranch while Randy—Blaine's best friend—owned and operated a bait and tackle shop in town. Mac Tolbert owned a ranch on the other side of Sunrise Bend. The six of them were close and all confirmed bachelors—well, except Sawyer. He had it bad for Tess.

A high-pitched laugh made him aware the ladies had resumed their conversation. Holly, Reagan, Tess and Erica formed a wall of women in front of him. Reminded him of those slumber parties his sisters used to throw, the ones where he and Blaine hid in their rooms to avoid detection and rarely succeeded.

He sidestepped away from them and carried the box over to the desk area. He didn't realize Holly followed him until he set it down and turned.

"You bought a baby swing?" Worry flitted through her eyes. "It wasn't on the list."

Wiping off his hands, he shrugged. "Mom and I expanded the list."

"But—"

"No buts. Clara needs this. You need it. Okay?"

"Oh, Jet." Erica's voice carried. He backed away from Holly and strode toward the door. Whatever his sister was about to say would only embarrass him. He was halfway outside when he heard peals of laughter. He shuddered. Way too many women. He could not get this stuff unloaded fast enough.

"Need help?" Erica asked as he came back in.

"No. I got it." For the next ten minutes, he brought in box after box. Then he took the new laptop off the passenger seat of his truck and brought it to Holly.

"Figured you needed your own." He handed her the box. Her pretty blue eyes grew round as her mouth opened slightly, drawing his attention to her pastel-pink lips. He quickly looked away.

"It's too much."

As he stared into her eyes, he wanted to tell her it wasn't nearly enough, but he sensed the other ladies had joined them.

"Jet, why don't you come over tomorrow?" Tess tilted her head. "Sawyer would sure love to see you. And, Holly, you should come, too, and bring the baby. I'd love to smoosh her little cheeks."

"Uh… I, uh…" What was wrong with him? He wasn't a stutterer.

"I have a better idea." Mom pointed to the boxes. "Jet, call the boys and have them come here tomorrow. Tess, bring Sawyer and little Tucker. Then they can all put together this stuff. I'll make a big batch of pulled pork, and Kevin can run to the store later for extra buns and chips."

"That sounds great, Julie. I'll make brownies." Tess nodded enthusiastically. "You'll call the rest of the guys, Jet?"

Yeah. Sounded real great. Now all his single friends would meet Holly—not that any of them were looking for a girlfriend, but her kind personality along with her pretty face would turn any guy's head.

"I'll call them." He gritted his teeth. This wasn't

what he'd had in mind when he'd thought about getting the guys together.

As the ladies began chattering about cookies and baked beans, he cast one more look at Holly, who watched him with questions in her eyes. If they were alone, he wouldn't mind answering them, but not here. He nodded to her, said goodbye to the group and walked out the door.

He'd better tranquilize his attraction to her. He had no right to feel possessive. He had no right to keep her from meeting his friends. And he had no right to want her for himself.

She was Cody's. He'd better not forget it.

This was too good to be true.

Holly changed Clara's diaper as Jet's friends laughed and joked and assembled the baby swing, a changing table, two sets of shelves, an Exersaucer and a bouncy seat. Erica, Reagan, Tess and Hannah Carr, one of Tess's and Reagan's best friends, all unpacked baby toys, stuffed animals and books. She couldn't believe Jet had purchased so much, and it humbled her to see all these people happily organizing the designated baby area next to her desk.

Last night she'd taken the laptop back to her cottage to install all the software Erica had said she needed. She'd been so excited, she'd actually started thinking in terms of living here permanently. But as soon as the thought hit, she'd gotten a panicky feeling and called Morgan, who'd once again urged her to move to Utah. Morgan assured her she could stay with her until she found her own place. Apparently, she'd met a great guy, too, and was keeping her eyes open for jobs Holly could apply for. It had been a good reminder she was only working here until she had enough saved to join Morgan and little Drake.

"Hey, Holly, where do you want this?" Jet approached as she finished snapping Clara's onesie. She pulled on her tiny purple stretchy pants.

Ignoring her racing pulse, Holly propped Clara on her hip. "What is it?"

"Uh…" He stared at the box in his hand. "A Pack 'n Play. I think it's like a portable crib or playpen or something. Mom said it was absolutely necessary."

Holly suppressed a laugh. "Once Clara gets a little bigger, it will be, but I've been managing fine without one. It helps that she's not moving around yet."

"Mom said she could nap in this."

True. It wouldn't be long before Clara would be too big to comfortably nap in her car seat.

"Why don't we store it until I need it?"

Clara twisted and held her arms out to Jet. His face softened. Holly never asked anyone if they wanted to hold the baby. They always asked her if they could. But Jet was different. "Want to hold her?"

His gaze searched hers and he nodded. "Yeah."

A shock rushed over her skin at the touch of his warm, callused hands. The baby snuggled up to him. He turned his head to smile at Clara, and all Holly could see was Cody. It was there in Jet's profile, in his lighthearted smile.

And it destroyed her.

Cody had never had a chance to meet his child. He hadn't even known she existed.

Not bothering to excuse herself, she walked as fast as possible to the bathroom, feeling Jet's gaze on her the entire way. As soon as she got inside, she locked the door, put the lid down and sat, shaking harder than a tree in a windstorm.

If Cody had lived, would he have eventually told her about his family? Would he have brought her here and introduced her to all of them? Would she have been as drawn to Jet as she was now? Or would he be just a nice brother-in-law, not the thoughtful cowboy she was starting to depend on?

A soft knock on the door forced her to take a deep breath and pull herself together.

"Be right out," she said.

She ran the water until it grew warm and held her ice-cold hands under it. Studied herself in the mirror. She looked healthier than she had in months, probably because she was sleeping better here. Even Clara was. She only woke up once in the night now instead of every three hours.

Okay. Get yourself together. It's normal to remember Cody and be sad. You're not a horrible person for noticing his brother. Jet's nice. You're just reacting to his kindness. When you're in Utah, you'll forget all about these uncomfortable feelings.

After drying her hands, she opened the door and returned to the showroom, where one of Jet's friends—Austin Watkins, a local rancher Jet had introduced her to—was relaying a story to Tess.

"Yeah, when I saw Tori's sister in town last night, it reminded me of that day when Tori went out on the ice. We told her it wasn't safe, but would she listen? No. And when she fell through? Man, my heart leaped out of my chest…"

Holly knew this one. Cody had told her about the girl who'd ignored their advice and walked out onto thin ice. How he'd jumped into action, raced to her and chipped the surrounding ice to drag her up, getting wet and chilled to the bone in the process.

"I still can't believe you sprinted out there the way you did. We were all standing around in shock while you're pounding your bare fists against the hole and dipping your arms in to grab her." Austin shook his head in awe. "You almost fell in."

Jet blushed. "Yeah, well, you and Mac held on to my legs when the ice gave way, and we all pulled her out. It was a group effort."

"No, that was all you, man." Mac Tolbert, another rancher about Jet's age, was shaking his head. "She would have drifted too far under the ice for us to grab her if it hadn't been for your quick thinking."

Holly blinked rapidly, her tongue darting over her top lip as reality shifted and their words sank in.

Cody hadn't saved the girl.

Jet had.

He was still holding Clara. He caught sight of her and edged out of the group, making his way over.

"I figured you'd want her back." His expression was full of affection for the baby. "Is everything all right? You look pale."

"You saved the girl who fell through the ice." She sounded as frozen as the lake, but she couldn't help it.

He flushed. "It was nothing."

"Did you get pneumonia?" She had to know what happened, how much of the story was true even if Cody wasn't the hero in it. Cody had told her he'd saved the girl and gotten pneumonia.

His jaw tightened. "Yeah, I did. How did you know?"

Those words told her everything. Cody had bragged about his brother's feat as if it was his own. And here stood Jet, embarrassed to have the story repeated.

He didn't want the glory.

"Just a hunch." She took Clara from him, startled once more at how little she'd known her own husband. She forced a smile. "Thank you, Jet, for all of this. You're making my life easier. But then, I think that's what you do, isn't it? You make everyone's life easier."

"I wouldn't say that." He stared at his feet.

"I would." She tilted her chin high. "You're one of a kind."

She'd thought she'd married one of a kind, and she supposed she had. Everyone was unique in their own way. But Jet…was different.

"Hey, Holly, can I hold Clara?" Tess's nose scrunched with a pleading expression, and Holly would have laughed if she wasn't so stunned by this new information about Cody.

"Of course." She handed Clara over without even a trickle of worry. At least her trust in people with the baby was slowly being restored. Her trust in men? Might never happen. Not after this fresh batch of revelations.

"Thank you! I've been dying to have this little

butterball in my arms since the minute I saw her yesterday." As Tess cradled Clara to her, Sawyer Roth, Tess's ranch manager and boyfriend, came up next to her, his eyes lighting as he stared at Clara. Tess looked up at him. "Isn't she precious, Sawyer?"

"Yes." A man of few words. But his eyes said it all.

"I've got to drag Holly away for a minute." Julie tapped on her arm and turned in the other direction. "Should we put the changing station in the hall next to the bathroom or *in* the bathroom, hon?"

"I don't know." Holly really didn't care where it went. "What do you think?"

"Well, if it's in the bathroom and one of us is in there, you might run into a problem, but if it's in the hallway…"

She listened with half an ear. She took in all of Jet's friends, his sisters, their friends and the space they'd set up for Clara near her desk. It had shelves and bins, a large play mat, the swing, the Exersaucer, the bouncy chair—and she felt an overwhelming sense of dismay.

She wished she could stay. Wished it would last. Wished she could slip into this family as easily as they made it seem.

But she couldn't. It wouldn't be long before the fantasy cracked.

She wouldn't lie to herself. She was falling too hard for the Mayers. Just like she'd fallen for her exes. Just like she'd fallen for Cody. And Jet, in particular, was wiggling into her heart.

How much of his attention was due to his responsible nature, though?

She might need them, but they certainly didn't need her. Jet included.

Chapter Six

~~◆~~

Jet tried to hide his yawn during the middle of a worship song in church the next morning. He'd been up since four, riding out on the UTV checking the cattle. A storm had begun around midnight, and he was glad all of the cows appeared to be fine. He and Blaine would ride again this afternoon. If the pastor would shorten the sermon by five minutes, he'd be able to get there that much sooner.

He shot a quick glance at Holly holding Clara on her lap next to him. Reagan was on Holly's other side, and Blaine sat next to Reagan on the end. Erica had driven to Jamie's earlier. The row wasn't big enough for the entire crew, so his parents were seated in front of them.

He really didn't want to be here today. Guilt brewed at the thought, but it was true. He had a million and one things to do on the ranch, and this weekend had been a bust at completing any of them.

"Please stand for the reading." The pastor motioned for everyone to rise. Jet got to his feet, steadying Holly's elbow when she jostled the baby.

"Our reading is from Matthew, chapter eleven. 'Come unto me, all ye that labour and are heavy laden, and I will give you rest. Take my yoke upon you, and learn of me; for I am meek and lowly in heart: and ye shall find rest unto your souls. For my yoke is easy, and my burden is light.'"

Rest? What was that? Jet shifted from one foot to the other. The heavy laden and labor he understood all too well. But the easy yoke, the light burden? Nope.

It was an odd word picture, anyhow. A yoke was placed around a pair of animals' necks so they would work in tandem, move in the same direction.

The last thing Jet needed was another restraint placed on him.

"If you're hesitant about giving up control, ask yourself if you're in step with the Lord." The pastor motioned for them to sit.

Am I in step with the Lord? The words seemed to echo and grow louder in his mind. He'd never thought about it. Wasn't sure he wanted to think about it.

Pssh. Of course he was in step with the Lord. He gave to church and did his best to be a good person. He'd sacrificed again and again to make the ranch succeed. Looked after his brothers, sisters and parents, and now Holly and Clara, too. What more was there?

The image of two animals yoked together came to mind.

Working in tandem in the same direction.

He couldn't remember the last time he'd questioned his direction. He did what was expected. Did what was best for everyone. Even Holly had alluded to it yesterday when she'd said he made everyone's life easier.

She'd made it sound like a good thing.

Then why didn't it feel good?

Clara let out a small cry, and Holly nudged him, whispering, "Mind if I slip past you? She's going to start wailing in a minute."

"Sure." He stood to let Holly pass. Clara's whimpers grew louder as Holly made her way to the back of the church. Jet wanted to look, to check they were okay, but he didn't want anyone speculating about them. As far as the town was concerned, she was family—Cody's family—and that was it.

He checked his watch. Ten more minutes and

he could go back to the ranch. Away from curious eyes. Away from the voice in his head telling him he hadn't been in step with the Lord for a long time.

"Thanks for driving us today." Holly glanced Jet's way as she buckled into the passenger seat of his truck after the service. Clara had fallen asleep after Holly had changed her diaper and fed her a bottle in the mothers' room. "I didn't realize we have another storm headed our way. I really need to get some formula and diapers. Do you mind stopping at the store on our way back?"

"Oh." He gripped the wheel with one hand. He smelled like balsam and lumberjack all wrapped up into one package. Clearly, it had been too long since she'd been in close quarters with a man, not counting when he'd driven her to Sunrise Bend for the first time. She'd been sick and hadn't noticed how he'd smelled. "Uh, sure."

Something in his tone alerted her he had better things to do than go shopping. Maybe she should have driven herself. But the winds had picked up, and her small car could have been blown off the road. Riding with Jet had been a smart move.

"We can head home if you'd like." She pressed the button for her seat to warm up. A girl could get used to the luxury of heated seats. "I can come back this afternoon."

"No, no. The winds will be too strong, and with the ice, I don't want you to chance it. I'll stop at Big Buck Supermarket." He turned in her direction to look back as he reversed, and she couldn't stop staring at his clean-shaven jaw. Everything about him seemed purposeful. Solid. Dependable.

Did he ever relax?

She thought back on his short visits throughout the week. He typically stayed for twenty to thirty minutes, and she always asked him what he'd done that day. At first, he'd brushed her off with a vague comment about checking cattle. She kept probing, though, and learned more about ranching and cows and how he spent his days. The cowboy life fascinated her for some reason. When he left, his face wouldn't be all hard angles. He even smiled sometimes.

"I understand if you need to get back," she said.

"Don't worry about it." His gaze met hers and her breath caught in her chest. He was a very handsome man.

He drove down Main Street past two-story buildings full of shops and businesses. Lampposts and awnings above recessed doorways gave it a charming feel. She looked forward to seeing it in the summer. Flowers would spill out of window boxes and people would stroll down the sidewalks. There had to be an ice-cream stand around here somewhere, too.

Why was she even thinking about the summer? She'd be gone by then. In Ogden. Her memories of the town had faded over the years, and the only thing that came to mind was the website full of photographs she'd clicked through.

Jet took a left into the supermarket parking lot. He found a spot and cut the engine. "Want me to stay out here with Clara? Or should we all go in?"

Holly bit her lower lip. What if Clara woke up and cried? He wouldn't know what to do.

"Let's all go in." She hoped he didn't think she didn't trust him. "I don't want you to have to sit here with a crying baby if she wakes up."

"Okay, I'll get the car seat." He got out, freed the car seat from the base and carried it by the handle as Holly came around to join him. When they entered the store, she found a cart and checked the signs to find the baby aisle. Jet stayed close by. "Do you need to pick up some groceries?"

She did. But in the truck, he'd seemed to be in a hurry, and she didn't want to put him out. "I can come back another time."

"Why not get everything now?" The sincerity in his deep brown eyes convinced her. "I've got time."

Since she'd already gotten her first paycheck

from Mayer Canyon Candles, she actually could buy groceries. Until now she'd been eating up the leftover food she'd brought from the apartment and having supper with the family at Kevin and Julie's insistence. She liked eating with them. She'd never been around a large, talkative family.

"Well, I haven't gotten groceries in a long time, but I'll do my best to make it quick." She steered straight ahead to the produce and quickly and carefully selected apples and bananas on sale. Then she inspected the vegetables and checked the prices before deciding what she needed. Some of them were terribly expensive in the winter. Canned and frozen veggies would have to suffice.

"I've never seen anyone buy groceries the way you do." Jet's eyes twinkled. He looked younger when he wasn't in serious mode. He usually was in serious mode.

"Oh, yeah? How do you do it?" She rolled the cart to the dairy section.

"I toss whatever looks good into the cart and hope for the best."

"How will you know how much it costs?" She'd been keeping a mental tally of her estimated total as she added items.

He shrugged, shifting the car seat to his other hand. "I don't."

"Well, there have been times I've had to put

items back when I was paying. It's pretty embarrassing, so I always add up the prices as I shop." Why had she admitted that? Now he'd think she was poor and helpless.

She'd never had much money, but she didn't feel poor. Or helpless. She'd been taking care of herself for almost eight years.

He didn't respond, and her cheeks were likely red as a tomato at this point, so she pushed the cart faster, adding eggs and milk to her haul. After selecting a few canned goods, bread and store-brand coffee, they made it to the baby aisle.

"Whoa." Jet stopped in his tracks. "Why are there so many choices?"

"I don't know." She found the brand of formula she used and rose on her tiptoes to find the exact container she preferred. "Why do they put things so high?" Using the bottom shelf as a step, she tried to hoist herself up enough to grab the canister.

Jet beat her to it. "You're going to break your neck." He easily plucked it off the shelf and handed it to her.

Show off. His dancing eyes made her smile. "Well, if they made it easier for us of more limited height to reach it, I wouldn't have to break my neck."

They stood inches apart and the air between them shifted, drew her to him. She looked into his eyes and all the bustle around them vanished. It was as if they were the only two people there.

What was she doing? Jet was off-limits. He was Cody's brother. Not to mention, they were in the middle of a crowded grocery store.

"Yeah. Okay. I'd better find the diapers." She tossed the formula in the cart and grabbed a few packages of diapers. Neither spoke as they joined the end of one of the checkout lines. Jet handed the car seat to her and moved to the front to unload everything onto the conveyor belt.

This was the first time she could remember not unloading her own groceries from the cart. And she liked it. She liked grocery shopping with Jet and having him reach for the high stuff and help her in the checkout lane. He made everything a little easier for her.

After the groceries were bagged and paid for, she made sure Clara, still sleeping, was safe in the back seat while Jet moved the bags to the bed of his truck.

He climbed into the driver's side and rubbed his hands together before starting it up.

"Thank you."

"Don't mention it."

"No, I mean it. I haven't had anyone help me in a long time. I'd forgotten what it's like."

"Well, you have a whole clan to help you anytime you need it. The Mayers are your family now, so if you need anything, we're here for you."

She sank back into her seat, filled with gratitude over the simple words. But as he backed out of the spot, she wondered what it cost him to be there for his family anytime for anything.

He had an awful lot to carry on those broad shoulders.

"You work a lot," she said. "What do you do for fun?"

He drove onto the road leading to the ranch. The wind gusted, causing snow to drift across the prairie and road. It didn't seem to faze him. "Fun? Oh, I don't know."

"You don't know?" His answer didn't surprise her, but it was kind of sad. "Well, what do you do when you aren't ranching?"

He kept his attention straight ahead and thought for a little bit. "In the fall, the guys and I get together for Monday night football. The season's over, though. In the summer, Blaine and I like to go camping near some hot springs not far from here. Austin and Randy usually try to join us. Mac even gets away from time to time. Maybe Sawyer will come this year now that he's back."

"The hot springs sound great, but camping? Doesn't sound fun to me."

"It is." He shot her a grin. "Are you worried about bears or something?"

"Yes, I am. Absolutely. I'm also afraid of sleeping on the hard ground. And snakes. And not having a bathroom." She'd never camped, but Morgan had regaled her with tales about her awful experiences, and it had made her never want to spend a single night in a tent. "What else you got?"

He focused on the road, and the silence stretched. It got to the point she didn't think he had anything more to say.

"What about traveling?" she asked. "You mentioned all those places you want to see."

"Haven't had the time yet." His jaw tightened.

"If I could go anywhere right now, it would be to a warm beach. Hot sun. White sand. Blue ocean." Snowy prairie spread out for miles. "I've hardly been anywhere."

"Do you want to travel?" He sounded curious. Surprised.

"In my dreams. Most days I have a hard time believing I'll even own a house at some point. Traveling would be whipped cream on a cup of cocoa."

"I know what you mean." He nodded. "I want to get out there, experience places, you know?"

Experience places. The phrase froze her. They were the exact words Cody had said to her.

Jet's words.

Like the other tale Cody had claimed for himself.

"Yes, I know," she said almost under her breath. She knew more about Jet than she should thanks to Cody. And she wished she didn't because, at the end of the day, it meant she'd married a complete stranger.

Who was the real Cody? Did she even care anymore?

She must be the most gullible person on the planet for marrying a guy she'd known for such a short period of time.

Jet might say she was part of the Mayer family, but deep down she knew she wasn't. Just like, deep down, she'd known rushing into marriage wasn't smart after trusting guys who'd claimed they loved her but had only brought her heartache.

This afternoon she'd run the numbers and figured out how long it would take to save up enough to move to Ogden. It was time to research the stores and boutiques that might be hiring and look into apartments.

In the meantime, she'd try to make Jet's life a little easier, the way he had hers.

He needed to check the cattle but wanted to stay in the warmth of Holly's cottage all afternoon. Jet set the diapers on the changing table in Clara's bedroom. Holly had hung framed pictures of pink bunnies on the walls. Besides the crib and dresser, a few toys and stuffed animals were stashed in a basket on the floor. It might not be a decorator's dream, but the room was girly. Sweet.

Just what he'd want if he ever had a baby girl.

He shook his head free of the thoughts. Thinking about babies? Had someone added drops of domestic fever to his coffee or something?

He returned to the kitchen, where Holly stood, holding the baby and scooping formula powder into a bottle. He found himself wanting to know more about her. He knew a little, but not much. No close family besides her cousin Morgan, no siblings. She wanted to move to Utah. She'd married Cody in a split second...

He had a lot of unanswered questions about Cody. Did she miss him? Had he been the love of her life? Had his brother been as much of a mess as when Jet had last seen him?

Had Cody been...happy?

Clara bounced on her hip and was getting fussy. Holly glanced at him. "Would you mind taking her for a minute?"

He took the baby from her. She squirmed and made grouchy noises. "You're hungry, aren't you? I understand. I get cranky, too, when my tummy's grumbling."

"All set." Holly finished testing the bottle and reached for Clara.

"I can feed her if you want." Now why had he offered that? He had cattle to check. And he'd never fed a baby before. Had fed plenty of bottles to orphaned calves, though. Couldn't be much different.

"Really?" She gestured to the living room. "Okay."

He was surprised she hadn't made an excuse to take the baby back. She'd definitely grown more comfortable with other people holding her child.

He carried Clara to a comfortable chair and cradled her in his arms. Holly handed him the bottle, and the baby reached for it, guiding it into her mouth as he held it. His heart squeezed with affection for the child. He looked up at Holly. "She's hungry, huh?"

"Yeah." Her soft smile set him at ease.

The questions about Cody pressed, forcing themselves to the forefront of his mind. "Do you mind if I ask you a personal question?"

Her eyes narrowed, but she nodded and took a seat on the couch.

"Did Cody seem to have himself together when you met him?" He held his breath, vaguely noting the gulping noises Clara made and the way Holly's expression brightened.

"Yes, he did." She got a faraway look, as if remembering something special. If he'd had any questions about how she'd felt about his brother, they'd been answered. And it reminded him he had no right to feel anything other than brotherly toward her.

He sat straighter, shifting Clara closer to him. Holly had shared Cody's final weeks, had known him better than Jet had at that point.

"Normally, I'd assume you already know this." Jet wanted her to know why they'd been estranged. Wanted to confess his guilt. "But given the fact that Cody told you he was an only child, I figure you don't."

"Know what?"

"The last time he and I spoke..." He shifted his jaw. "It wasn't good."

"I wondered about that," she said quietly. "Why would he hide all of you from me?"

"It had been a good six months since we'd spoken." Should he tell her everything? Her eyes—sad, expectant—locked with his. He'd better tell it to her straight. "Cody was high energy. Always looking for fun and adventure. The kid scared me when he was young. He took so many risks. Had the attention span of a fruit fly. But he was pretty special."

She crossed one leg over the other, watching him intently.

"He didn't really take to ranching." Jet could admit it now. They'd tried everything to help Cody find his niche here, but they'd failed. "He helped here and there, then threw himself into competing in rodeos for a while. Then he just kind of quit everything. Started keeping odd hours. Smelled like alcohol and weed more often than not. Dad warned him to get his act together or bear the consequences."

Her eyes grew round as he continued, "I'm not trying to put him down or to change your feelings about him. I loved him. We all did. I figured you'd understand why he hid us from you if you knew what led up to his moving away from here." He might as well tell it all. She deserved to know why Cody had disowned them. "It was me. I'm why he disowned us all. The last words I told him were if he wanted to waste his life smoking pot and getting drunk, fine, but he needed to do it somewhere else. He left the next day."

She folded her hands and stared at them on her lap. Clara's body grew heavier in his arms, and he noted how groggy she appeared as she continued to work the bottle half-heartedly. Her sweetness filled his heart. But he knew he'd hurt Holly's.

"That makes more sense." Holly worked a kink out of her neck. "If it makes you feel better, he didn't drink or smoke anything when we were together. He did highway maintenance and talked about wanting to move up to a better position. And, yeah, he was high energy. He seized the day. I liked that about him."

Each word was a relief and a burden. Knowing his brother had gotten cleaned up and had figured out his place in life took away some of his guilt. But hearing Holly talk about liking Cody's adventurous personality deflated his ego.

Jet was the opposite of adventurous. He was reliable. Boring.

"Was he happy?" He couldn't keep the pleading out of his tone.

"Yeah." Her face cleared as she smiled. "We were happy."

We were happy.

Of course, they were. And he was a fool sitting there holding his brother's baby, drawn to his widow, looking for some sort of redemption. Something that would make it acceptable for him to move on from Cody's death and explore more with Holly.

"I'm glad." He practically choked on the words. "I worried…well, I feared…"

"You don't need to worry, Jet," Holly said. "I think he found himself after leaving the ranch.

I hate that his life was cut short when it held so much promise."

"I do, too." To his horror, tears threatened to spill. Rising slowly to not bother the baby, he set Clara in Holly's arms. He wasn't sure if he could speak without breaking down. So he swallowed a few times and finally gave her a nod. "I've got to go."

Her gaze questioned him, but he pivoted and strode to the door, swiped his coat off the hook and left.

Out in the fresh air, he gulped in a few breaths. Then he strode toward the stables where his life made sense and he could concentrate on things like cattle and hay and horses. Things that didn't break his spirit.

His little brother had been ten years younger than him, and he'd had a fuller life than Jet had ever managed.

Jealous of his dead brother. He couldn't imagine anything lower than that.

She should have told him.

Holly held Clara, still sleepily drinking from the bottle now and then, and fought the growing guilt clenching in her chest.

She'd told him the truth about Cody. He *had* been happy. His life had been together. He'd never touched alcohol or cigarettes or weed or anything else in her presence, and she'd never detected it on him, either. He'd been excited about his job.

But he'd also kept secrets.

Told stories about himself that weren't true. He'd stolen Jet's heroic moments, and it left her with conflicting emotions.

She'd needed to hear why Cody had cut his family out of his life. Needed to know. Jet's explanation made sense. Cody was a hothead. He'd yell one minute and grin the next.

His family might not realize it, but their tough love had clearly impacted him for the good. He just hadn't recognized it in time to give them credit.

Did they need to hear it from her?

Or would it drive a wedge between them? She didn't want to cause the family more pain by bringing up a sore subject.

The bottle rolled out of Clara's open mouth as she fell asleep. Holly carried her to her room, set her in the crib and covered her with a light blanket.

As much as she hated that Cody had lied to her, she wouldn't have done anything differently.

He'd given her Clara. For that, she'd be eternally grateful.

She went back to the living room.

Jet had seemed to be overcome with emotion

before he'd left. He'd loved Cody, too. They all had. And that was partly why she'd kept a few things to herself just now.

She didn't want him to think even worse about Cody than he already did. If Jet knew his brother had claimed all the things he'd done as his own, he might get upset all over again. And it was best for everyone if they all made peace with the fact that Cody was gone. They had their own lives to lead.

Yeah, right. This isn't about Jet's peace. It's about you.

Her? Hardly. She snatched her phone off the counter and started scrolling through it as her hammering heartbeat convicted her.

You like Jet. And part of it is because you thought Cody actually did the things he'd claimed. But Jet was the one who'd done them.

Yeah, well, so what? So she had a tiny thing for her brother-in-law. She was prone to crushes. Had been her entire life. Didn't mean she was going to act on it. Not this time, anyway.

He didn't need to know Cody had stolen the best parts of his identity. Didn't need to know she'd liked hearing Cody's tales of the ranch. The ones that were actually Jet's.

Jet didn't need to know she liked his tales of the ranch, too—the ones he shared with her when he stopped by each night.

Even if getting close to Jet wouldn't be extremely inappropriate, she was done jumping into relationships at the snap of her fingers.

It was time to come up with a plan. Life on her terms. Without the crushing consequences of giving her heart to people who thought they wanted it but later decided they didn't.

Chapter Seven

As much as she tried not to become too invested in Mayer Canyon Candles, she couldn't help loving her job. Holly had been working there for three weeks already. She wanted to define the company's brand in a unique way. Over the past several days, after putting Clara to bed, she'd mocked up new labels for the candles. She'd also created graphics to use on the website and to increase their presence on social media sites.

Would the Mayer ladies appreciate her ideas?

She scrolled through her presentation one more time after lunch. Her days here had flown by in a flurry of working, researching potential jobs and apartments in Ogden, figuring out a savings plan to move there, watching Clara roll over for the first time and spending time with Jet each evening.

He insisted on checking on her and Clara

every night. It was her favorite part of the day. She didn't want to think about why. She simply enjoyed it for now. He'd already warned her he wouldn't be seeing much of anyone as soon as calving began in earnest, which would be happening soon. Too bad. She was under the impression he enjoyed sharing his day with her as much as she did with him.

Tess was officially doing the bookkeeping and had dropped by last week, showing off her pretty engagement ring. Sawyer had popped the question. Erica, of course, had squealed. Reagan had begged to hear every word he'd said. And Holly had stood nearby, happy for Tess but a little sad, too. She'd thought getting married would be the beginning of an amazing life, and it had ended for her almost before it began.

Still…she had so much to be thankful for. Holly glanced down at Clara in her bouncy seat next to her desk in the showroom.

Lately Julie, Erica and Reagan had been wrapped up in wedding planning when they weren't fulfilling candle orders. Holly enjoyed listening to them discuss the catering, dress fittings and invitations, but it also made her feel a bit left out. This week Erica was at Jamie's dealership, though, so this was as good a time as ever to get Julie's and Reagan's attention.

"Ugh, leave me alone, Mom." Reagan glided

through the workshop door toward the kitchen with Julie on her heels. "I'm not going to date Dan just because he's the best man and I'm the maid of honor."

"I didn't say you were." Julie wiped her hands on her work apron as Reagan thrust a mug into the microwave.

"You implied it." Her big hazel eyes blazed as she turned and leaned against the counter.

"Well," Julie huffed. "You're not going to find a date if you're here all the time. I think you kids need to have people over more often. Like when everyone set up Clara's things a few weeks ago. It was nice having Mac and Randy and Austin here. They're all single. Any one of them would make a good husband."

Reagan shifted her attention to Holly and mouthed *Help me*. Holly fought back a giggle.

"I'm not interested in Mac or Randy or Austin, and they aren't interested in me, either."

"I wouldn't be too sure about that." Julie pursed her lips. "They are all fine-looking fellas, and they have their acts together. Your dad would be over the moon if you fell in love with a rancher like Austin or Mac."

Reagan closed her eyes, her nostrils flaring as she took quick breaths. "Well, he's going to have to stay under the moon, because it's not happening."

"Just keep an open mind. That's all I'm asking."

The microwave beeped and Reagan took the mug over to Holly's desk. She crouched to smile at Clara, who grinned and kicked her little legs. "You're such a happy baby. And so cute. You might be the cutest baby on the planet."

Holly's heart filled to bursting. It did every day. Because every day, multiple times, the Mayer women loved on her little girl.

"One of those could be yours, Reagan," Julie practically crooned. "Just set your eyes on one of those local boys…"

Reagan rose, leaning in to Holly. "Please get her off my back. I don't know why she's obsessed with me getting a boyfriend today. I can't take much more."

It was the perfect moment to show them her ideas. But part of her balked. She didn't want anything to jeopardize the time she had here. Even if it was only a few months.

"Weddings are so romantic…" Julie's voice matched the faraway look in her eyes.

Reagan stiffened. Holly took pity on her.

"Do you two have a few minutes?" Holly asked.

"Sure," Reagan said. "What do you need?"

"Let's go over to the counter where we can all sit." She closed her laptop and placed it under her arm as Reagan unbuckled Clara and carried her to one of the stools at the counter.

Holly settled into the middle stool with Julie on one side and Reagan with Clara on the other. She clicked on the slide presentation with the graphics.

Before she began, she glanced at Reagan then at Julie. "Just to warn you, I've been looking at job openings in Ogden, Utah, where my cousin lives. While I was researching, I came across several really cute boutiques, and it gave me ideas for the candles."

"You're still planning on moving?" Reagan asked as she lightly bounced Clara on her lap. "Why don't you stay? We like having you here."

She liked it here. Felt like she kind of belonged with them. Or, at least, that she could belong with them.

"I hope you're not going soon." Julie covered Holly's hand and gave her a sad smile.

"Oh, no. I have to save up first."

"Well, don't hurry. I know it's not easy missing your friends and family. If you're serious about going, though, we should probably hire someone part-time soon." Julie tapped her chin. "When you decide to move, we'll switch them to full-time."

"That's a good idea." Holly tried to be pleased because it *was* a good idea, but it was also a painful reminder how easy it would be to replace her. She wasn't indispensable. Sure, they'd miss her and Clara when she was gone, but their lives would go on the way they had before.

She, on the other hand, doubted her life would ever be the same after being wrapped up in the Mayer family. It had given her a glimpse of a life she'd never thought possible. One with common goals and people to rely on. She was really going to miss this place.

"So what do you have?" Reagan pointed to the screen.

"Ideas. For your brand." Holly met Julie's eyes then Reagan's. They seemed open to what she had to say. "I love what you've done with the company. I'm just making suggestions on how to make your products really stand out."

"Let's see what you've got." Julie waved her fingers toward the laptop screen.

Holly took a deep breath. *Lord, please let them take this the right way.*

A sense of calm washed over her. No matter what, God was for her.

She clicked on the presentation.

"Your candles are beautiful. Carefully made. Full of rich, vibrant scents and colors. I sold similar candles for years at the store I worked for. And I think with a few tweaks to their presentation—specifically the labels and names—these would be hot sellers in gift boutiques across the country."

"Boutiques?" Julie frowned, rubbing a finger under her eyes where her glasses hit. "How would we get them into boutiques?"

"Well, I think you could start by increasing your social media presence. Rework the website. Push the Etsy store. Make sure every graphic, every label, every part of your brand matches and points customers back to Mayer Canyon Candles."

"I'm not in love with our current labels." Reagan shrugged, kissing the top of Clara's head. "We agreed on them, but I think they could be better."

"I mocked up some new designs. More illustrative ones. Mind you, these aren't perfect, just ideas on what direction you could go." She clicked through to a pale pink label with a calligraphic illustration of a peony with the words *Peony & Prose.* "I thought of the new scent combination you created, Reagan, with the peony base and hints of pepper and violet, and I pictured an English country home with a library and garden. The label tells a story complementing the scent."

Reagan leaned in to study it. Then she glanced at Holly with astonishment. "It's exactly the scent. *Peony & Prose.* It's perfect."

"You like it then?" She hadn't dared hope they'd be on board right away.

"I love it." Reagan peered around her to Julie. "We could do this with all the scents."

"It's…" Julie blinked a few times. Holly cringed. Would she hate it or love it? "Elegant. So much better than anything we came up with." She beamed at Holly. "Do you have more?"

"Yes." Holly clicked to the next label, Weekend Cuddles, with the sketch of a woman holding up a puppy. "This one is—"

"Cozy with all the feels." Reagan's face lit up. "The bergamot and musk. It's fantastic!"

"Holly, could you do this for all the candles?" Julie asked.

"Yes. I mean…it would take a while, but yes." They wanted her to redesign all the labels? Exactly the reaction she'd craved.

"When we started the business, we were focused on getting the product right. Well, the product *is* right—but the presentation is lacking." Julie's eyes sparkled. "This is what we need. Would all of the labels be pale pink?"

"I don't know." Holly hadn't thought that far ahead. "I think some would look better with dark labels and metallic lettering. I guess it would depend on the candle itself."

They spent the next thirty minutes bouncing ideas off each other as Holly clicked through the rest of the presentation, including her ideas for the website and social media ads.

"Holly, I know you have your own plans," Julie said. "But I hope you know we'd love to have you here permanently. There is always a place for you at Mayer Canyon Candles if you change your mind about moving."

Gratitude hit her hard. Julie meant it. And Reagan's enthusiastic nod confirmed it. She wished she could stay here forever. Clara would have a warm, loving, extended family to rely on, and she'd have a job she adored.

But would it last? Experience told her no.

"We'd better get cracking on those vanilla soy candles, Reagan." Julie stood. "Oh, Holly, Jet texted me earlier that we had our first calf. That boy forgets to eat during calving season. Would you mind dropping off a plate of supper to him later for me? It would save me the trip."

"Of course not." Holly stood, too, gathering the laptop.

"Come around six. You can eat with us first. Kevin's making a feast."

"Okay, I will."

"And, Holly?" Julie paused.

"Yes?"

"Thank you for all your hard work. Cody was blessed to have you. And we are, too."

Her emotions had been all over the place,

and this kindness was the breaking point. Holly pressed her lips under and nodded. Then she excused herself and fled to the bathroom.

This family made her want to stay. But she'd given her heart away time and again, only to have it dismissed.

She couldn't handle becoming an afterthought of the Mayers. And Julie might think she was pining over Cody, but Holly had been thinking about Jet more than him for quite some time. Would Julie still be so accepting if she knew Holly's true feelings? Would Jet?

She didn't plan to stick around to find out.

He'd missed one. He was sure of it.

Jet rubbed the towel over his damp hair then pulled a sweatshirt over his head. Nothing like a hot shower and clean clothes to revive a guy after hours in the saddle checking pregnant cows. He mentally backtracked through the day, picturing the tags he and Mateo, one of the ranch hands, had sought out. Blaine and Jim, a seasoned cowboy in his early sixties, had ridden out to the opposite pastures.

He and Mateo had checked dozens of cows earlier, and the very first calf of the season had been born. He had a feeling at least two more would come tonight. Instinct and years of experience gave him a special sense when it came to calving. That's why his brain was nagging him about missing a cow.

But which one? He was sure he'd checked them all.

A knock on his front door broke him free of the thoughts. He padded on bare feet through his bedroom, down the hallway, past the living room to the foyer. There, on the front step, was Holly, holding a bundled-up Clara on her hip and a plastic bag straining with containers dangling from her hand.

"I brought food." Her shy expression captured him, as did the ribbons of blond hair streaming from beneath the gray stocking cap she wore.

With his mouth as dry as the salt licks he put out for the cattle, he stepped aside and ushered her in.

"I know you're tired." The dip between her eyebrows was adorable. "Your mom asked me to drop this off."

"Ah... I'm not surprised." His lips spread into a lazy grin, and he didn't care to think too much about why he always felt like smiling when she was around. One thing he knew—he didn't want her to leave yet. "Keep me company while I eat?"

Her face cleared and she nodded. "Okay."

She took off her coat and Clara's one-piece snowsuit while he piled a plate high with fried chicken and mashed potatoes. They sat opposite each other at the table. A fire crackled in the fireplace of the living room, and the country music station he'd turned on earlier played in the background.

"I hear your first calf was born today." Holly bent to the side to get a few toys for Clara, who sat on her lap, slapping the tabletop with her tiny, chubby palms.

"Yes. The next couple of months are going to be wild." He shoveled in a bite, enjoying the way the glow of the light complimented her skin.

"Wild, huh?" A playful smile teased her lips. "How wild are we talking?"

"Two to three hours of sleep at a time. Cowboys taking shifts to check the pregnant cows we think are ready to give birth. Thinking on our toes, tagging newborns, freezing in our boots and hoping the weather doesn't kill any of the herd."

"My job sounds like paradise compared to that."

"I couldn't work in a building all day." He tore off a piece of biscuit and popped it in his mouth. Chewed and swallowed. "Sitting at a desk indoors is not my style."

"Sitting at a desk indoors is definitely *my* style."

"I'm glad to hear it. How's it going over there?"

"Really good. I ran a few ideas by your mom and sister today, and it looks like we're going to rebrand the candles. New labels. Overhaul the website. That sort of thing."

"Your idea?" He shouldn't be surprised, but Holly constantly surprised him. He was seeing new dimensions to her all the time.

"Yeah, why?" Insecurity twisted her features, reminding him she'd grown up very differently than he had. Opinions were spoken loud and often in his family, whereas she might not be used to sharing hers.

"I think it's incredible. I can't wait to see what y'all come up with." He continued eating. Clara took a squeaky ring-shaped toy and began gumming it, making a loud humming noise in the process.

"What's your family like, Holly?" He kept getting the feeling she knew him better than he knew her. Sure, she was a devoted, caring mom, a gentle spirit, smart, hardworking and kind. But he didn't know what had made her that way.

"My family?" She let out a fake laugh. "There's not much to say."

"It won't take long, then, will it?" he teased.

"I suppose not." Her sad smile stole all the way to his heart. Maybe he shouldn't be asking personal questions. He was already growing too close. "I grew up in LaGrange with a single mom. My dad left us when I was three. I don't have a relationship with him. Mom remarried and moved to North Dakota the summer before my senior year. I moved in with Morgan to finish high school in LaGrange. Made milkshakes and fries after school to pay my portion of the rent."

Jet turned his attention to the dwindling food on his plate so she wouldn't see his shock. She'd basically been on her own at seventeen?

"Why didn't you move to North Dakota with your mom?"

Her face pinched. "We don't see eye to eye. And I don't like the man she married."

"Why not?"

She shrugged. "I got a weird vibe from him."

His muscles tensed. It took a lot of willpower to keep from clenching his hands into fists. The thought of any guy giving Holly weird vibes made him want to make sure said man never laid eyes on her again.

"Morgan is two years older than me." Clara dropped the toy, so Holly handed her a small, stuffed green frog. She promptly shoved its leg in her mouth. "She's fun. More fun than I am, that's for sure."

"Why do you say that?"

"Morgan's never afraid to try something new. She hated her job, so she took a chance and moved to Ogden. And she's really happy there."

He swallowed an uncomfortable sensation. How many chances had he taken in life?

Holly continued, "As soon as I graduated from high school, I got a job at a drugstore. It wasn't long after I found out the bath and body store in Cheyenne was hiring. Morgan was serious about her boyfriend at the time—they decided to move in together. So I got a cheap place of my own. Worked hard. Got promoted. Morgan got pregnant with Drake, her boyfriend left her and she threw herself into a new job. She's always been outgoing. I met Cody at one of her gatherings."

His brain screeched to a halt at his brother's name. In thinking about her past, he kept overlooking the Cody factor. He pushed his empty plate to the side. Clara took the moment to yawn, her little arms rising above her head.

"That's probably my cue." Holly shifted the baby.

"For what?"

"This is when she has a bottle and falls asleep. I'd better take her home."

He didn't want her to go home. He wanted to hear more about her life. The one before Cody, at least.

"What if I warmed a bottle for you?" he asked. "Would you stay awhile?"

Surprise flickered in her eyes. "I don't know. You need your sleep. Aren't you getting up in a few hours to check all those cows?"

"I can never sleep the first couple nights of calving. My mind races in circles wondering which ones I missed."

"I know the feeling. Not the cows, mind you. But I've spent a lot of nights chasing thoughts and never quite catching them."

"So stay." He tilted his head and shrugged. "Distract me from the cows. I like hearing about your life."

"You do?" She ducked her chin briefly. "If you really want me to."

He did. He found himself wanting to know everything there was to know about her. Even if it meant hearing about her life with Cody. Maybe it would help the facts sink in—she'd loved his brother. There was no place in her heart for him.

So stay. Two simple words that meant more to her than he could possibly know. After her lonely childhood, it still surprised her when other people wanted her around. But his final words had really twirled batons and streamers over her heart. *I like hearing about your life.*

Did anyone like hearing about her life?

Had anyone ever asked?

Not even Cody had been all that interested in it, if she were being honest.

Jet stood and carried his plate to the kitchen sink. "Do you have a bottle? I'll warm it up."

"Actually, I do." She didn't go anywhere without a stocked diaper bag. "I'll change her into pajamas while you warm the bottle."

In seconds she'd unearthed the purple-striped pajamas with flying cows printed all over them. Silly things. How she'd miss these baby clothes when Clara outgrew them.

"You can change her on my bed if you'd like." His fingers brushed hers, making her breath catch, as he took the bottle. "Down the hall to the left."

She nodded her thanks, carrying Clara and the diaper bag to his room. It consisted of a large bed neatly made with a navy blue comforter, two dressers and a television. Everything was orderly. Making quick time of it, she changed Clara's diaper and got her into the pajamas. When she returned, Jet had taken a seat in the leather chair near the fireplace, so she sat on the couch across from him. She wrapped Clara in a baby blanket and gave her the bottle.

"When did Morgan move to Ogden?" Jet sank back in the chair, propping one ankle on the opposite knee. His relaxed pose was so striking, Holly's mouth went dry. She forgot he expected a response.

"Oh, um, recently." She looked down at the baby, her lids already drooping.

He frowned. "You said she has a child, too, right? Drake? How old is he?"

"Yes. He just turned two. He's a cutie. A whirlwind of energy, but he sure is adorable." She'd learned about infants from spending time with Morgan and him.

"If you move to Utah, how can you be sure Morgan will stay?" He didn't sound judgmental, but she tensed. She didn't know. And until now, she hadn't allowed herself to think about it.

"She's really happy there. I talked to her yesterday. She's got a good job and an apartment near shops and restaurants."

He opened his mouth to say something, but she didn't want to discuss Morgan anymore tonight. "How is the whole 'splitting the ranch with Blaine' thing going?"

"Uh, good." He drummed his fingers on the arm of the chair. "Actually, it's not."

"Going good?"

"Going at all."

"You're not splitting the ranch?"

"We are. It's just…stalled."

"Oh." She watched the firelight dance on his face.

"It's been busy." He wiped his hand over his mouth. And met her eyes again.

"I'm sure."

"And I don't know if Blaine is ready."

"Huh." She'd watched Blaine over the past weeks. He was more laid-back than the rest of the bunch, but he got things done. "He seems reliable."

"He is," he said quickly. "Blaine's the best guy I know."

"But you don't trust him?"

"It's not a matter of trust."

"I guess I don't understand." She should keep her mouth shut. Here she'd wanted to change the subject to something safer, and she was botching it.

"He's never been in charge. He doesn't know what it's like to have the weight of the entire ranch on him. I make all the tough decisions. I don't want to see him struggle."

"Struggle is part of it, though."

"Part of what?" His gaze trapped hers. It wasn't an angry skewer, more like a fascinated hold. One she liked.

"Becoming who you're supposed to be. It makes you stronger. Strong enough to make the tough decisions. To bear the weight of the entire ranch."

He seemed to chew on her words. "I don't want him to have to go through what I went through."

"Like what?" She leaned forward to set the empty bottle on the coffee table. Clara had fallen asleep in her arms.

"Making big decisions without a clue if I was choosing correctly. Dad always gave me advice, but this year…" He shook his head. "I've had to figure it out on my own. Selling calves. Keeping heifers. Deciding on a new bull. Having to put down a good old cow who'd spent her entire life on this ranch. Bottle feeding a calf for days only to have it die, anyway. Making sure the ranch has enough income to support everyone. Rotating pastures. Finding a dead calf in the middle of the night and wondering if there was anything I could have done to save it."

"Oh." She hadn't realized he dealt with all those things. "It's a big job. But Blaine isn't a little boy anymore."

"I know." He turned his attention to the fire, his profile the picture of seriousness. "We'll get it sorted out. Expand and utilize all our property better, too."

"And he'll have you to talk to when he needs answers to the tough questions."

"I suppose."

"It's not easy. When I have difficult decisions to make, I pray and remind myself God is for me. I'll pray for you, too."

"Holly…" The intensity in his eyes burned, glowed, and fizzy adrenaline spiked through her veins. She knew the precise instant she needed to leave. If she didn't, she'd go and do something stupid like stand and fall into his arms. And from the gleam in his eyes, she figured he wanted the same.

"I'm taking this little one to bed," she said, rising.

The intensity in his gaze snuffed out, and he rose, too.

She handed him the baby while she got her coat and boots on. Then she took Clara back, hiked the diaper bag up on her shoulder and turned to leave.

"Holly?" He kept his hand on the door. She turned to look at him, all too aware the handsome cowboy was inches from her.

"Yes?"

"Would you mind bringing supper over tomorrow night, too?" The vulnerability radiating from him slayed her. If she didn't know better, she'd think he was lonely. That he needed her company as much as she needed his.

And that couldn't be right. He was surrounded by family and friends.

"Of course." She gave him her brightest smile.

No way he needs you. No way he's lonely. Don't make more of this than it is.

"Good night, Jet." And she left.

She'd bring him supper for as long as he asked. And she'd bring him something more. An ear to listen. The man *did* have too many responsibilities. Helping him with his burdens was one small way she could repay him for his kindness. If she didn't read more into it, she'd be fine.

Chapter Eight

"Calving is killing me." Austin Watkins flopped onto Mac's couch, his head tipping back to stare at the ceiling. "It's times like this I get why you don't want to ranch with me, Randy."

"You love every minute of it." Randy grinned at him then turned his attention to Jet. "Hey, I brought the book I told you about."

"What book?" Jet asked. He and the guys were sitting around Mac Tolbert's massive living room Friday night. Whenever the six of them got together, they usually came here. Mac had the most room—and the best snacks.

"The house plans." Randy stood. "I keep forgetting to drop it off. It's in my truck. I'll go get it."

"You're finally getting serious about building a house, huh?" Mac asked Jet. "Never thought I'd see the day."

"Yeah." Jet glared at him. What was that supposed to mean?

"I'll believe it when I see it," Blaine muttered.

"What about you, Blaine?" Austin asked. "Where are you going to live once you guys get the ranch figured out?"

"Grandpa's house. I'm renovating it first. In the meantime, I'm moving into Champ's place. Cleaned it up this week." Blaine cast a sideways glance at Jet. Champ had been Grandpa's ranch foreman for years. His modest three-bedroom home was near the outbuildings at Grandpa's place. It, too, had sat empty for far too long.

"I didn't know that," Jet said. A sensation he couldn't quite identify raised his hackles. He knew everything going on at the ranch. It was his job to know.

But he hadn't known about this.

He shouldn't be surprised. Ever since Holly's comment about the struggle making you stronger, Jet had been taking a long, hard look at himself, and he didn't really like what he was seeing.

She was right. He'd been treating his brother like a little kid, not a grown man.

"Yeah, well I don't need permission from you." Blaine lifted one shoulder in a shrug.

"I didn't say you did." He only had himself to blame for Blaine not telling him. He needed to smooth things over with him soon or he wouldn't have any brothers left.

Blaine made a snorting sound as if to say *Yeah, right.*

"Randy's foundation is being dug in a few weeks," Austin said. "Soon as the ground thaws. Hate to admit it, but I think I'm going to miss having him around."

The two of them lived in the old farmhouse where they'd grown up. Both their parents had died years ago, leaving them the ranch.

"He won't be far." Mac took an enormous bowl of popcorn from the coffee table and set it on his lap.

"Twenty minutes." Austin made it sound like it was in another state.

"Yeah, but he'll be close to the store. Plus, his property backs up to a wide stream." Blaine reached over to palm a handful of popcorn. He and Randy had always been close. "As much as he loves to fish, he couldn't have asked for a better spot."

An uncomfortable thought occurred to Jet—had Blaine told Randy he was moving into Champ's house? Jet was usually the first to know.

"It's just going to be different," Austin said.

"Different doesn't mean bad." Sawyer's tone was serious. It usually was. His years away from

Sunrise Bend had been tough on him. Tess was slowly bringing out his more playful side.

"I'll help you move your furniture this weekend, Blaine." Jet didn't want this rift between them to get any wider.

A confused expression clouded his face. "You will?"

"Yeah. I should have asked you about it sooner."

"You should have?"

"You turning into a parrot or something?" Austin teased.

"No, I've gotten used to being put off." Blaine addressed Jet. "What's going on with you?"

"Look, I know we need to split the ranch, and if calving wasn't taking up every minute, we'd be further along." An uneasy feeling crept through his body, though. What if he was wrong? What if they split everything and Blaine couldn't handle running his half? If Jet called him out on it, would he get mad and cut him out of his life the way Cody had?

Now where had that thought come from?

"Here you go." Randy returned with the book. He plopped down next to Jet on the couch. "Here, I'll show you the plan I chose."

Randy leafed through the book until stopping at an attractive two-story home. Jet let out a low whistle. "Wow, that is something."

"You like it?" he asked.

"What's not to like?" Jet studied the floor plan, asking him questions as they discussed the layout. "Will the back of the house face the river and mountains?"

"Yeah. Can't wait to wake up to that view. I'm having a deck built across the entire back to enjoy it."

For an instant, Jet envied him. Randy was living for himself. Making plans. Building a house.

What would it be like to do what he wanted? Not what everyone else needed?

"That's a big house for one guy." Mac's eyes twinkled. "You sure there isn't a girlfriend lurking in the shadows we don't know about?"

They all laughed and watched Randy. His face turned red, but the set of his jaw confirmed what they all knew. "No. No girlfriend. My future involves the store and fishing. Not a wife. No kids, either."

"I hear you, brother," Austin said, raising his hand for a high five. Mac and Blaine joined in, too.

"Uh-oh, looks like Jet's being awfully quiet over there," Mac teased as he pointed to him.

"What?" Had they all figured out he couldn't get Holly and Clara off his mind? "Girlfriend? Nope. Not me." He stuck his nose in the book of house plans. All of them begged for a family.

Why build a house with four bedrooms if they'd sit empty? "If you want to talk weddings, Sawyer's your man. I'm up to here—" he raised his hand over his head "—with wedding talk from my sisters and Mom."

"I keep forgetting Erica's getting hitched." Austin shook his head. "It's a shame. She was one of the few women in this area who kept my interest. She's a fireball."

"Hey, that's my sister," Jet and Blaine said in unison. Everyone chuckled, including them.

"I can't help it if your parents produced hot daughters."

Jet glared at Austin. "If you so much as look at Reagan, I'll—"

"Relax. I'm teasing you."

Jet glowered at him long and hard. It wasn't that he was opposed to any of his friends marrying Reagan. It was just…he preferred life the way it was. With her single. And him not worried about a guy's intentions toward her. Including one of his friends.

He had a hard time seeing her as old enough to get married. To him, she'd always be the shy high school freshman afraid to attend the homecoming dance. He'd driven her himself, told her she was the prettiest girl there and if any guy said otherwise, he was a moron.

"So, Sawyer, when's the big date?" Blaine

asked. "I still think you should have dressed in camo and gone on a hunt for the engagement ring."

"No offense, but that was the dumbest idea I'd ever heard," Sawyer said. "And, no, Randy, before you even ask, I didn't cast a fishing pole with the engagement ring on the hook."

Randy's face fell.

"We're getting married this summer. Early July. And I'm formally asking all of you to be my groomsmen. Austin, I need you to be my best man."

"Of course." Austin's grin was a mile wide.

"Honored." Randy nodded.

"Absolutely," Blaine and Jet said simultaneously.

"Can't wait." Mac grinned.

Jet, listening with half an ear as the conversation shifted to the upcoming start of the MLB season, resumed leafing through the book of house plans.

Sawyer had taken a chance on love. Randy was building a house. Even his own brother was taking charge, fixing up the home rightfully his.

Maybe Jet didn't have to put his life on hold anymore. Maybe he could find a way to have some of the things he wanted while running the ranch and making sure the family was okay. It was something to think about.

* * *

Saturday morning Holly carried the laundry basket of warm baby clothes to the living area where Clara bounced in her seat, clutching a rattle. Sunlight fell in thick stripes on the carpet. What a lovely, sunny day for late March. She grabbed the pajamas on top of the pile and began to fold them. Clara was outgrowing her clothes. Holly had been putting off buying new, but she was going to have to do some online shopping soon.

Last night she'd reviewed her bank accounts, double-checked her budget and realized she was getting closer to her financial goals than she imagined possible in such a short time. Of course, the Mayer family's generosity was the reason. She didn't pay rent, and she was earning an hourly wage two dollars more than what she'd earned at her old job. Having few expenses also made a huge difference.

She folded a onesie. She'd been checking the apartment prices in Ogden. There weren't many available. She should probably figure out a realistic monthly payment. It would affect how soon she could move and what kind of salary she'd require.

The thought of moving to Utah didn't fill her with anticipation the way it had in the past. Not that she'd ever been giddy about moving. It had felt more like a way out of the problems she'd found herself in. An escape, even. A good one.

Her phone rang. She tossed the shirt back in the laundry basket to answer.

"Hello?"

"I have good news." Morgan's vibrant personality added pep to her tone. "The bath and body franchise you worked for is opening a new store near the historic district downtown! You *have* to apply."

Her heartbeat sped up. She'd worked at the chain for five years. She knew it inside and out. But she'd been fired from the previous store. Would the new one even consider hiring her? "When is it opening?"

"I'm not sure. I noticed a construction crew there all winter, but it wasn't until yesterday I found out what store was moving in. There's a Coming Soon sign. I'll keep an eye out for a Now Hiring sign, okay?"

"Yeah, that would be great. Thanks, Morgan." She'd check out the historic district online later. It sounded inviting. And it couldn't hurt to put her application in. "How is Drake?"

"Hyper as ever. He's watching cartoons at the moment. Cam's coming over later. I can't wait for you to meet him."

"I should be able to move this summer."

"That long? You can always move in with me until you find a place. It will be great."

This wasn't the first time Morgan had offered her space in her two-bedroom apartment, but Holly had lived with her before and didn't want to again. Morgan loved having people over. Holly liked her privacy. A two-bedroom was too small for four of them, but even if Morgan had a huge apartment, Holly needed her own place.

"I have things I need to take care of before I move there." It was true. She needed to find a job, although Morgan's tip might have taken care of that problem, and she needed to train someone to take her place here at the candle company. So far, Julie and Reagan hadn't even tried to hire someone else. Her mood dampened. "I'm not sure when I'll be able to get away."

A few moments ticked by before Morgan replied. "You like it there, don't you?"

"I do."

"That's good. I mean… I'm happy for you."

"But?" Holly could hear it dripping silently off Morgan's tongue.

"But these things don't typically work out, do they?"

"What things?"

"In-law things. Family businesses. Outsiders. Some people are really good at making you think they want you around. And then the next thing you know, they're taking you for granted, and you realize you were a novelty. It's happened to both of us. Don't deny it."

No, she wouldn't. Words bubbled up from her throat to defend the Mayers—Julie and Reagan, Erica and… Jet.

"I'm happy for you, Hols. Really, I am. But if it feels too good to be true, it probably is."

It did feel too good to be true. Impossibly good.

"Thanks, Morgan. You've always been here for me. I'll always be here for you, too."

"I know. We'll always have each other's backs."

"That's right."

"I'll keep an eye out for a Now Hiring sign."

"And I'll let you know when I have a better timeline to move down there."

They chatted for a few more minutes before hanging up. Holly finished folding the clothes as Clara began to fuss.

"What's going on, peaches?" She lifted her out of the bouncy chair. "Feeling restless?"

Her tiny face puckered and she let out a half-hearted cry. Thinking back to Morgan's words, Holly was tempted to let out a cry herself.

Her cousin was right. This was a too-good-to-be-true situation. And it wouldn't last.

In fact, it had been showing signs of cracking

for a while. Reagan and Julie had been preoccupied with calls from Erica all week about the wedding. And Holly had taken supper over to Jet every night, but twice he'd almost fallen asleep at the table across from her. She'd chalked it up to a temporary shift in everyone's priorities, but maybe it was the beginning of the end.

They'd all included her and made her feel like part of the family since the minute she'd arrived. Was the novelty wearing off?

She'd better discuss finding a part-time employee to replace her. If the store in Ogden hired her, she didn't want to leave Mayer Canyon Candles in the lurch.

The first of April arrived with a vengeance. This entire day had felt like one bad April Fools' joke.

Jet ducked his chin firmly into his chest as cold rain pelted him on his way to the barn that evening. Last night he'd taken the midnight shift, riding around the pasture on the UTV, not seeing any signs of cows delivering calves. Then he'd gotten a call at three in the morning from Mateo that one of the pregnant cows was in labor but something didn't seem right. So he'd driven out there and spent what felt like forever waiting for the first-time mama to have the calf.

He'd had to drive the calf to the shed, put it in

a warming box and then bring it back to her. It had taken some coaxing before it would nurse. Thankfully, they both seemed to be doing okay.

But he'd only gotten an hour's nap, and since then, there'd been a birthing bonanza. Had every cow on the ranch decided today was the day to have her baby?

A colder, more miserable day, they couldn't have picked.

All he wanted was a hot shower, a warm meal and his bed. In that order.

Well, not quite. He wanted to listen to Holly's chatter while he ate. He'd been so tired yesterday, he'd almost fallen asleep while she told him about the labels she'd designed for Reagan's new scents. He'd been interested, too. Usually, he didn't get all that excited about the candle business, but hearing her describe it made it alluring.

She probably thought he was a jerk or that she was boring him. Nothing could be further from the truth.

He was simply tired.

He opened the barn door and strode to the office as he shook the rain from his hat. After scanning the spreadsheet he kept on all the cows, he scrawled a list of tags for Mateo to check that night. Was he forgetting any of them? He didn't know, and he was too exhausted to care.

A light in the stables behind the barn caught

his attention. His part-timer, Colin, mucked stalls. Jet checked his watch. After six thirty. He usually let Colin off duty at six, but unfortunately, calving meant more work for everyone.

"Why don't you go ahead and take off." He met the skinny kid's eyes. Colin was graduating from high school soon. Worked hard. Never complained.

"Okay. Should I come early tomorrow?"

Jet tried to think of what was happening tomorrow. What day was it, anyhow?

"Last Saturday you told me to wait until noon."

Oh, it was Friday. Right. "Noon will be fine. I hope you're hanging out with friends tonight."

The kid blushed as he propped the pitchfork against the stall. "Yeah. Gigi Hollis is having people over."

"Gigi, huh?" Jet knew the family, but not well.

"Everyone's going. She and Aiden Cox broke up this week. She told me I should come over tonight." He blinked, frowned and then shrugged. "I've got nothing else to do."

"You like her?"

His face grew brick-red. "Yeah, she's cool."

Jet wouldn't torment the kid. He clearly had a thing for Gigi. "Well, have fun. I'll see you tomorrow."

Nostalgia filled him as Colin left, and he finished mucking the stall. He remembered the anticipation of going to parties in high school. He'd done everything with Austin, Mac and Sawyer. Randy and Blaine usually joined them, too. He missed the carefree days when all he'd had to worry about was school and chores and girls.

Once he finished, he jogged through the rain back to his cabin. Inside he flipped on the lights, stripped off his wet jacket and beelined to the shower. Fifteen minutes later he was dressed and on the couch in front of a freshly lit fire. His eyelids drooped, but he kept propping them up to peek out the front window.

Would Holly bring him supper tonight as usual? Or would Mom drop it off?

Holly might have plans. It was Friday, after all. His sisters could have dragged her to town for pizza. Or she might be relaxing in the cottage, enjoying some well-earned rest.

Just because he couldn't wait to see her every night didn't mean she felt the same way. He'd practically forced her to come over. And he didn't know why.

He'd never been one to need his hand held. He carried out his duties and gave out orders. So why was he pulling a Colin and Gigi here? Playing it cool in his head in case Holly didn't come over. In case she didn't like him the way he liked her.

He closed his eyes. She had no reason to like him that way. He was her brother-in-law, and his mom had put her up to bringing food over because his mom wanted him to eat. That was all.

He probably should find out if Blaine needed more help at Grandpa's place. Last weekend, they'd moved the rest of his furniture and belongings into Champ's house. Then they'd toured Grandpa's home. The place was a seventies time bomb.

It had been unsettling, helping him move. Made the upcoming split more real.

Dad and Blaine wanted the ranch divided. Jet had been balking. And it hadn't helped anyone.

The pastor's words from a few weeks ago must have lodged in his brain because, more and more, he felt like he was in step with the Lord regarding the ranch. Now, Holly, on the other hand…

A knock on the door launched him to his feet. He opened it.

"Slight change in plans." Holly's lopsided smile didn't quite hide the questions in her eyes. "Hope you like pizza."

She held a white box he recognized from Dino's. And she didn't have the baby.

"Where's Clara?" He opened the door wider as she ducked under his arm inside. Her light perfume about knocked him out in the best possible way.

"Your mom and dad are watching her."

"Are you okay with it?"

"I wouldn't be here if I wasn't." She set the box on his kitchen counter and opened it. "They're wonderful with her, and she loves being with them."

"Wouldn't you rather have some time for yourself?" He followed her, inhaling the aroma of pepperoni.

"Why? Do you want me to go?" Her stricken expression told him he was a fool.

"No, I was hoping you'd stop by."

"You were?"

"Yeah." He tucked a section of her stray hair behind her ear, luxuriating in the silky softness. "I don't want to monopolize your time."

"You aren't. I like coming over, like hearing about your day."

"When I don't fall asleep." He grimaced then opened a cupboard for plates.

"You only nodded off once." Her smile kicked the dust off his sense of humor. He chuckled. "Okay, twice."

"Well, it isn't a reflection of the company I'm with."

They sat at the table and began to eat.

"Did you have more calves today?" she asked.

"Yeah, and then some." He told her about the calf in the night and about how he'd then driven from one group of cows to the next as they dropped babies left and right. She laughed when he mentioned the entire herd getting together and planning it to make his life miserable. Something about her laugh unraveled some of the tension gripping his insides.

"So now that you know way more about calving than you ever wanted to, what's going on with the candle biz?" He finished off another piece of pizza and watched as pride and elation danced across her face. He liked seeing her happy.

"Well, the labels I mentioned? I'm close to being done. Reagan and your mom only had issues with three of them, and I was able to tweak the designs to their liking. Tess knows a website guy who will revamp the site for us. Beyond that, Erica's wedding plans are moving at full throttle."

"They aren't working you too hard, are they?" He searched her face for signs of burnout. Aside from the puffiness under her eyes, she looked great.

"No, but we all agreed we need to hire someone part-time."

"I've been telling them to hire more employees for months. Maybe they'll actually listen to you."

"Well, this is more so they can prepare for when I leave."

He stilled. Holly hadn't mentioned leaving in a few weeks. He'd hoped—foolishly—she'd like it here enough to ditch her plans to move to Utah.

"Have you decided when you're leaving or something?" He tried to keep his tone neutral, without much success. Exhaustion started to weigh on his bones.

"No, but Morgan told me there's a store opening soon. The same chain I worked for in Cheyenne. When they start hiring, I'm putting in my application."

He leaned back as thoughts circled like buzzards. "I thought you liked it here."

"Oh, I do," she said brightly.

"Then why leave?" He didn't understand. Couldn't pretend to understand. She had a comfortable home, a good job, a family—why would she turn her back on all this?

"I hope you don't think I'm ungrateful. It's not that. It's just…" She wiped a napkin over her mouth, keeping her gaze averted. "This isn't my home. Not really."

"What are you talking about?" He twisted his neck until it cracked. The lack of sleep was adding a bite to his words he didn't intend. "This is your home. Yours and Clara's."

"You all got on fine without me before. You'll get along fine without me again."

It was true, but he didn't like it. He didn't like thinking about her and Clara in a strange town. Or in a dumpy apartment like the one he'd found her in. Or strapped for cash. Or sick with no way of paying to see a doctor.

No, he didn't like the thought of her anywhere but right across the lane in Grandma's cottage.

His cell phone rang and he answered it immediately. "Hello?"

"I can't locate the red tag number 73," Mateo said. "Did you check on her earlier?"

That's what he'd been forgetting. She was the cow he'd missed. Curling the fingers of his left hand into his palm, he tightened his grip on the phone in his other hand.

"No, man. I forgot. I'll come out now—"

"That's all right. Blaine's driving up. Sorry to bother you. I'll let you know what we find." The line went dead.

He'd gotten distracted, and it might cost him a good breeding cow. A calf, too. Should he leave it to Mateo and Blaine? No, they didn't know the gullies she and her buddies hid in. He stood abruptly.

"Is everything all right?" Holly's face pinched with concern.

"No, it's not. I missed a cow, and I've got to go back out there. That's what I get for being distracted."

She looked like she'd been slapped. "I'm sorry I distracted you."

"That's not what I meant." Maybe it was. She'd been distracting him since the day he'd met her.

His phone rang again. Blaine. "What?"

"Mateo told me about the cow. Don't worry. I checked on her an hour ago. She had the calf. They're both doing fine."

"Why didn't you let me know sooner?" he practically barked even though he knew he was being unreasonable.

"You didn't ask." His voice rose. "What's your problem? I took care of it. It's more than I can say about you." And Blaine hung up.

The blood drained from his face as he slowly lowered the phone to place it on the table.

"I couldn't help overhearing." Holly stepped toward him. "Don't blame yourself. It all turned out okay."

He was so irritated, he couldn't speak. The trouble was, he didn't know who he was more furious with. Holly for trying to smooth things over. Blaine for taking care of an animal Jet should have tended to. Or himself for being such a jerk to everyone involved.

"When is the last time you slept?" She set her hand on his arm, and the touch stilled all the noise in his head.

"I don't remember." All the fight leached out of him.

"Come on." She led him by the hand down the hall. "Let your brother handle it. Get some rest."

She stopped in the doorway of his bedroom and gave him a gentle push. "Sleep."

He let go of her hand, turning back to look at her. No one, except his mother, told him what to do. No one but Holly could have convinced him to stretch out on his bed and get some shut-eye.

"You didn't distract me, you know," he said before crawling on top of the bed and promptly falling asleep.

Chapter Nine

The next morning during Clara's nap, Holly typed in another search for apartments in Ogden. The prices, though similar to Cheyenne's, were still pretty high, and only a few places were available. Were they in good areas? From what Morgan had told her, Ogden was a safe place to live. But every town had its share of crime.

For the first time, she faced the unpleasant facts she'd been ignoring. The worst one being she'd have to find a babysitter for Clara. No retail store would allow her to bring a baby to work. Morgan would help, but she worked full-time, too.

She'd be forced to hire a stranger to watch her child.

Just thinking of it felt like two hands were gripping her throat. How could she be sure they wouldn't neglect her? How would she know her baby was being loved? At the very least, cared for properly?

As icy spears of panic spread up her chest, she closed the laptop and shoved it to the side. No use getting all worked up. She'd call Morgan about potential sitters. She'd have options when the time came.

Last night something had shifted between her and Jet when she'd told him to rest. Maybe she was the only one who'd felt it. But she knew he'd been happy to see her on his doorstep, just as she knew he'd allowed her to order him to get some sleep because he trusted her.

The man was a fighter, but he only seemed to be fighting himself. And watching him give this ranch his all made her want to share some of his burden. Take a tiny bit from him so he could regroup, get his strength back, the way he'd helped her get hers back.

A knock on her door made her jump. She hurried to it.

Jet arched his eyebrows and grinned.

"What are you doing here?" A rush of happiness filled her.

"Apologizing." His eyes shimmered with appreciation.

"For what?"

"For ruining a perfectly good Friday night."

"You didn't—"

"I was grouchy and rude and I fell asleep." He opened his hands in a helpless manner. "Forgive me?"

She couldn't help but chuckle. "There's nothing to forgive."

"I just finished my shift. Want to take a drive?" He held up his keys. "It's not far."

The air hinted at spring. Blue skies, sunshine and everything soggy. "Clara's sleeping."

"We can wait for her to wake up."

Holly thought of her plans for the day. She had none besides ordering bigger clothes for the baby, and that could wait.

"Come on in." She waved him inside. As if on cue, a cry came from the back bedroom. "Looks like she's awake. Make yourself at home. I'll be right back."

She padded down the hall and picked Clara up. Sweat matted her fine brown hair in little curls around her forehead. "Mama's here." She kissed her head, cradling her to her chest. "Let's get you changed."

As Clara snuggled close to her, she hoped she would always remember these moments. Her baby was growing up so quickly.

It didn't take long to change her diaper, and then Holly carried her back to the living room, where Jet had perched on the edge of the couch, knees wide, hands clasped between them.

"Hey, there's our little princess." He stood, closing the distance, and Clara held her arms out to him. "You want your uncle Jet?"

He took her in his arms. *Our little princess.* The sight of him, so similar to Clara's daddy, made her lungs seize. Jet was a strong man. A rugged cowboy. And as tender as could be with her baby girl.

"Does she need to eat or anything?" He looked over Clara's head to Holly.

"Not for a few hours. Let me grab my coat and we can go."

Ten minutes later Holly stared out at the beautiful vista as Jet's truck came to a stop at the end of a muddy lane on the ranch. "Where are we?"

"This is where I've decided to build my house." He opened the door and climbed out. "Hold up, I'll come to you. It's muddy."

She waited for him to open the passenger door. Pivoting, so her feet were on the runner, she assessed the ground. Wet. To her surprise, Jet put both hands around her waist and lifted her out of the truck. He spun her as if she weighed nothing and set her on a small mound of yellowed grass.

The touch of his hands on her waist sent her heart fluttering. He gave her a tender smile, his lips so close to hers, she could feel his hot breath. She stared at his mouth, then his eyes, then anywhere else.

She wanted him to kiss her.

His velvet eyes made her consider leaning in. The way his hands lingered, she figured he wanted the same thing. Finally, he let go. "Wait right there. I'll get Clara."

Seconds later, he held the baby, wide-eyed and making babbling noises, and joined her.

"You're looking at the site of my future home."

"It's a good spot." She looked around, noting the creek in the distance, the mountains far away. A stunning view from any angle. His parents' house and the ranch buildings were visible across the prairie, too. What would it be like to have land and a new house with plenty of room?

"It is." He nodded with an air of satisfaction. "And it's close to the barns and outbuildings, but not too close."

"Same with your parents' house. Close, but not too close."

"Exactly." He grinned, keeping his grip on Clara.

"When are you going to start building?"

"I'm still looking at house plans. Randy lent me his book and recommended a local contractor."

She couldn't remember ever seeing Jet look this free, this happy.

"Of course, it will take a long time. I have no idea when I'd even break ground."

"Well, after you pick a house plan, you can figure all that out." She couldn't help picturing a pretty house here with her and Clara rocking on the front porch. "I guess this means you and Blaine have ironed out the details concerning the ranch."

His forehead wrinkled. "We're working on it."

"Your mom told me Blaine moved to the original ranch. It's not too far, right?"

"Yeah, five miles, give or take. I helped move some of his furniture last weekend. He plans on renovating Grandpa's house."

"What else do you have to do?"

"To his house?" he asked.

"No, silly, the ranch."

"This half of the ranch is in my name. The other half of the property is in Blaine's. It's really a matter of repairing his outbuildings, installing a few new corrals and dividing the cattle. We'll need to purchase a few more bulls and keep more heifers. Our income will likely decrease this year to account for the split."

"Are you worried about money?"

"We have plenty of reserves. We'll be fine."

"You're obviously too busy to do any of that right now." She stretched her neck to take in the full view. "Are you thinking this summer?"

"I don't see how we could get it all done by summer."

"I didn't mean to just divide the cattle and be done. You said yourself the outbuildings need to be taken care of."

"Yeah, they do. I just…" He stared into the distance.

When he didn't continue, she stepped off her little hill to the wet ground next to him. The moisture seeped into her athletic shoes. "What is it?"

"How do I know it won't hurt our relationship?" He faced her then, his eyes full of questions.

"Blaine? The thought never crossed my mind."

"I watched one brother fall apart when things got hard."

Cody. Of course. Why hadn't she put it together?

"Cody and Blaine are opposites, Jet." She wanted to help him understand but wasn't sure what he needed to hear. "And Cody may have fallen apart, but he also got his life back together. He talked about his faith to me. God was watching out for him."

Jet shifted to face her again. "Watching out for him? By letting him die? Just when he'd found happiness…with you?" The final two words were so low she almost didn't hear them.

"I don't like it, either, Jet, but we all die at some point."

He faced the mountains again, his profile thoughtful.

"What kind of house are you looking to build?" Maybe a lighter subject would be best. "A one-story? Two-story?"

His face cleared like the sun coming out from behind a cloud. "Two-story. It doesn't have to be a mansion, but it needs to feel spacious. I've liked coming home to my cabin, but it's cramped. I'm ready to spread out."

"What about the layout?" She loved going through one of the apps on her phone to search through home ideas. Someday, maybe, she and Clara would have a home of their own.

"What about it?"

"Well, do you want an open floor plan? And have you thought about the kitchen? Dark cabinets? Light cabinets? Or white cabinets? And the flooring—carpet or tile or hardwood? There are so many things you'll get to pick out."

He went a bit green around the gills. "Hardwood. For sure. I don't know about the rest. I might have to get some help with that."

"You have sisters and a mom who would gladly give you input."

He shuddered. "Yeah, I'll be full up on their opinions whether I want them or not."

"I won't argue with you there." She laughed. "I know it's squishy, but do you mind if we walk around a bit? I feel like it's been ages since I've spent more than two minutes outside."

"I'd like that. Come on. I'll show you around." He still held Clara in one arm, and he offered the other to Holly. She linked hers with his. "This way. See those trees over there? There's a creek running behind them…"

As she strolled on Jet's arm, listening to him point out details about the land she never would have noticed on her own, she cherished every moment. She could listen to him talk about prairie dogs, pronghorns, pine trees and creeks forever. And when they stopped near a pile of rocks with native tall grasses growing around them, Jet grew quiet.

"Is something the matter?" she asked.

"No. I just…this spot always gets to me."

"Why?"

He handed her Clara then crouched, looking toward the horizon. "Our dog, Buddy, came across a rattler here when I was younger. I saw the snake and I saw Buddy barking, and it all happened so fast…"

He shook his head and straightened. Holly held her breath, knowing where the story was going. She could picture it all in her mind. Cody with the shotgun. The rattlesnake about to strike.

"My hands were shaking so badly, I was sure

I was going to hit Buddy." He inhaled deeply, then met her eyes. "I prayed the fastest prayer on record, and God listened. The bullet hit the snake, not the dog."

Her entire body went still. Not Cody... Jet. Like the girl falling through the ice. Like the ring Cody had given her. All. Belonged. To. Jet.

She'd known. Of course, she'd known. Why did she keep pretending *any* of Cody's stories were really his? They weren't.

"Were you valedictorian of your class?" she asked, knowing the answer but needing it confirmed.

His face flushed. "Yeah, why?"

"And Cody?"

"Valedictorian?" He looked taken aback as he let out a disbelieving laugh. "No, he didn't like school much."

Just as she'd suspected.

While old stories weren't the entire reason she'd fallen for Cody, they'd been part of his appeal. The real Cody wasn't who he'd led her to believe he was.

She looked at Jet, still upset years later from having to make a snap decision that could have killed his dog, and she knew the truth.

She'd married the wrong brother.

She'd been in love with Jet all along.

* * *

Was this what love felt like?

Jet couldn't think straight as he ripped carpet from the corner of the living room in Grandpa's—Blaine's—place later that afternoon. Showing Holly the site of his future home had changed something inside him. Maybe it had been her arm linked with his. Maybe it had been her baby in his arms. Maybe it had been the feel of his hands on her waist as he'd lifted her out of the truck to avoid the puddles.

Whatever it was, he was in trouble.

He'd almost kissed her.

What a disaster that would have been. Kissing his sister-in-law? The one with Cody's baby? Who worked with his mom and sisters? Who lived precisely thirty yards away from him?

"Hey, easy." Blaine looked over from the other corner. "I don't want the floorboards coming up, too. What's got you all bothered?"

He supposed he'd been a bit hyper since arriving. He had all this energy winding him up and no idea what to do with it.

"I've got a grip on it now. Ready to pull?" Jet asked him. Blaine nodded. They heaved on the carpet and rolled it away from the tack strips holding it down. Sweat beaded above his temples as they knelt to roll it across the room. Next, they pulled up the old pad and rolled it up, too. Then they each took an end of the carpet and carried it outside to the dumpster Blaine had rented. The pad followed.

"What's next?" Jet returned to the kitchen where Blaine took two sodas out of a cooler and tossed one to him. He cracked it open and drank half the can.

"The den." Blaine grimaced, taking a long drink. "I need a break, though. It's been a long day."

"Long week."

"Long month."

They met each other's eyes and grinned.

"So what's the deal between you and Holly?" Blaine asked.

Jet spewed out his drink mid-sip, spraying it on the counter. "What?"

"Mom said she's taking supper to you each night. And I saw you together earlier at the spot where you plan on building."

"Mom coerced her into bringing me supper." He wiped the counter with his sleeve. Blaine's eyebrows rose. "And I figured she doesn't get out much and might want some fresh air." Wow, that sounded lame.

"Uh-huh." His brother wasn't buying a word he was saying. "It's okay, you know. She's pretty cool. I don't blame you for liking her."

"I don't like her." The words came out garbled.

"Yes, you do."

"She was Cody's wife." Jet gave him a pointed stare.

"Yeah, and she's not anymore."

"She would be."

"But she's not." Blaine gave him the *are you stupid* look he'd perfected over the years. "Cody died. There's nothing we can do about it now. Do you think she should stay single forever or something?"

Yes.

Blaine gave him the side-eye. "I don't care what the guys say about not getting married. Now that Sawyer's taking the plunge, another will follow. Mark my words."

"Are you saying one of our friends should date Holly? Marry her?"

Blaine shrugged. "I'm not saying anything. Any single guy would have to be blind not to notice she's single and pretty. Mac and Austin are your age. They might be thinking about having families of their own."

"Not with Holly!" He regretted the outburst instantly.

Blaine's mouth curved into a slow grin that said *I told you so.*

"Look, I don't have time for a relationship. I've got the calves to think about and Erica's wedding and getting these outbuildings fixed up and finding a house plan and…"

"Whatever you say. You're *real* involved with Erica's wedding plans and all."

Jet wanted to wipe the smirk off his face.

"Speaking of outbuildings…" Blaine said. "Why don't we take this outside and give them a quick look-see. You always find things I miss and vice versa. We'll write down everything that needs to be done."

Jet held back the *no* on the tip of his tongue. He didn't want to inspect the outbuildings. He didn't even want to help Blaine fix this place up.

He wanted everything to stay the way it was.

But Blaine was already halfway out the door. Jet had no choice but to follow him.

They spent a long time touring the buildings. Blaine jotted everything down in a little notebook he kept in his back pocket. When they finished, they returned to the kitchen.

Jet's head swam with the repairs they needed to hire someone to do, the equipment they'd need to purchase. Both his and Blaine's phones chimed at the same time. He checked his phone. A text from his mom came through. Don't forget you boys need to get fitted for your tuxes tomorrow.

He groaned. He'd forgotten about the stupid tux fittings. They'd have to drive over an hour to get to the rental shop. And it was almost time for him to go back out and relieve Mateo of his cattle duties.

"Want me to drive tomorrow or you?" Blaine held up his phone.

"I'll drive."

Blaine was right. He did like Holly. And the guys around here were sure to come calling soon. He had way too much to deal with to add a romantic entanglement to the list.

If Blaine had noticed he liked Holly, the rest of the family wouldn't be far behind.

She wasn't staying, and she wasn't his.

Without overthinking it, he texted her. No need to bring me supper anymore. I'll be helping Blaine fix up the house.

There. Problem solved. He'd see less of Holly, help Blaine with the house and be in better shape to divide the ranch when the time was right.

So why did he have an uneasy feeling? Like he was going in the wrong direction?

He wouldn't dwell on it. But he couldn't help thinking if he was really doing the right thing, why did he feel so miserable?

Monday morning Holly carried Clara to the workshop door and peeked inside. "Do you two have a minute?"

"Sure. We're almost done with this batch,"

Julie said as Reagan reached up on tiptoes for a box.

Good. Because she needed to train a replacement soon, and neither of them showed any interest in hiring someone.

Erica breezed into the showroom, shrugging off her coat as soon as she was inside. "Brr...it's cold out there. I've always thought winter storms should be outlawed in April. And half the time we get them in May, too. I should talk Jamie into moving to Florida."

Holly nodded. "I'll join you."

"Would you?" Erica put her arm around Holly's shoulders. "We need to get away from here. Somewhere warm and fantastic with sunshine and a pool."

She could picture it, and it sounded amazing.

"I finally convinced Jamie about the honeymoon." Erica set her purse on her desk, sat and took out a day planner and pen. "I'm booking us a week in St. John later this summer."

A honeymoon. How she'd love to travel somewhere for a week with no worries.

"St. John the island?" Holly lowered Clara into the Exersaucer nearby. As soon as her tiny feet touched the bottom, she was bouncing and making gurgling sounds.

"Yep. I can't wait for my toes to sink into white

sand." She closed her eyes and sighed. "I can practically smell it."

The workshop door opened, and Reagan and Julie joined them. "What do you think of the new scent, Beachy Keen?"

"Ooh, I like it." Erica nodded enthusiastically. "It's like I'm smelling my honeymoon. By the way, the caterer got back to me. We can decorate the night before."

"Oh, good. I'll tell the boys they're staying an extra night." Julie pulled out her phone, squinting behind her glasses as her fingers tapped out a message.

"Like you'll be able to drag them away from their precious cattle for two whole nights." Erica shook her head.

"This is a wedding." Julie lifted her finger. "Their sister. They *will* leave the cattle."

Holly twisted her hands together. Lately, every time she tried to bring up something business-related, the three of them were so deep into wedding plans, they barely paid attention to a word she said. She needed to buck up and be firm this time.

She was moving on, and if they didn't hire someone soon, they'd be unprepared.

They were obsessed with the wedding. Jet was busy helping Blaine each night. And she was left on the outside, longing to get in.

"Um, I was wondering if you'd found anyone to hire?" Holly held her breath as each woman turned to her with a confused expression. "We've talked about me training someone."

"No, it's been the furthest thing from my mind." Julie shrugged good-naturedly. "I can barely keep my head on straight with the candle orders and the wedding."

"I'm not good at hiring people." Reagan looked positively terrified. "Or firing people. I'm more of the worker bee."

"Don't look at me." Erica brought her hands up to her chest. "These hands are full."

"Well, I'd be glad to place an ad and put the word out around town." She faked a bright smile. "It will take some time to train someone."

"Would you?" Julie sighed in relief. "That would be a big help."

"You don't mind?" Erica caught her eye. "I'd feel better knowing this place was fully staffed before I move. I have to say, hiring Tess to do the bookkeeping and having you in charge of everything else on the business end, including the marketing, has been a huge blessing."

"Oh, I agree," Reagan said. "With you here, Mom and I can concentrate on what we do best."

Holly savored their kind words, tucking them away to remember later. "So, you're okay with me looking?"

"Honey, I'm okay with you looking, hiring, training—the works." Julie spread her arms out. "We'll tell you if we aren't sure of someone."

"Great. I'll get right on it." Holly made a mental list of everything she'd need to do to hire someone. "What kind of hours and pay are you thinking?"

But Reagan and Julie were already looking over Erica's shoulders at her laptop. Holly glanced at the screen. Flower arrangements.

She sighed. Her wedding had involved a five-minute perusal of the wedding chapel's packages in Vegas. And she hadn't cared because as long as she was with Cody, she was happy.

As much as she liked being part of this family and business, she was slowly becoming invisible.

She'd been an afterthought too many times in the past. She couldn't become one again.

If he got one more text message about setting up tables for Erica's upcoming bridal shower, he was going to lose it. Jet sat in the ranch office and added three more calves to the spreadsheet Wednesday evening. This had been one of their best seasons yet, and they would continue to have more calves for at least another month. The wedding and calving had done nothing to take his mind off Holly, though, no matter how much he tried.

He set down his pen, arched his back and took in his office. Memories of sitting in here with Dad drifted back. How much he'd anticipated being in this chair—the boss's chair—one day.

But he hadn't fully grasped it would mean Dad wouldn't be out here anymore.

How much of this past year had been about missing Cody? And how much had been about missing having Dad out here?

He'd left a big chair to fill.

Was Jet worthy of it?

He was trying to be. That had to count for something.

He slid the spreadsheet into a folder and placed it in the drawer. He and Blaine had been making a lot of progress on the house renovations. They'd decided to wait a few weeks when they were less frazzled to start taking bids on fixing up the outbuildings. Their relationship was back to normal. Better than normal, really.

But he missed Holly.

It had only been a few days since they'd stopped eating supper together. It felt much longer.

He liked telling her about his day. Liked the way her eyes sparkled as she listened, the questions she asked. Liked hearing about what she was doing at the candle shop. Liked being with her.

Did she miss him, too?

Jet drummed his fingers against the desk.

He'd slammed the door on their spending time together for no good reason.

That wasn't true. He had his reasons.

He'd been growing too close to her. And he was too busy, had too many other things to deal with…

Too scared.

He wiped both hands down his cheeks and blew out a breath. He was too scared to give his heart to her when she'd given hers to his brother. His risk-taking, fun-loving brother. What would she ever see in old, reliable Jet?

He turned out the lights. Strolled through the barn, noting everything was in its place.

Even if she did see something in him, he had no right to pursue anything with her. She was a young widow, a new mom trying to create a life for her child. The last thing she needed was an unavailable workaholic like him.

Chapter Ten

It was time to get some much-needed rest. Holly sank into the couch after a long day of work and fed Clara her bottle. The past two weeks had gone by so quickly, she wouldn't be surprised if she had whiplash. At least it was Friday. The entire weekend loomed ahead of her, empty and inviting.

It had taken a week to interview, hire and start training Sadie Lyon, a married mother of three looking to get back in the workforce now that her kids were all in school. Sadie was a quick learner and appreciated the fact that she could take off early for sports practices and wasn't locked into working weekends. She was already well on her way to taking care of all the administrative work, including helping with the special packaging method. It left Holly free to concentrate on marketing and product design.

Not that she'd be doing either much longer.

In six weeks, she'd saved enough money for a deposit on an apartment, the first month's rent and enough to pay utilities and groceries for a while if she kept to a tight budget. A couple more weeks of saving would provide the cushion she needed.

And then it would be time to move on.

Clara took greedy gulps of the bottle, one hand curled around it, the other reaching up for a fistful of Holly's hair. The sweetheart was tired. She'd woken early from her afternoon nap for some reason and had been extra active while Holly researched print services that would produce a quality label at their price point.

Reagan and Julie were so preoccupied with filling orders and planning Erica's bridal shower, they'd barely glanced at the designs she'd been working on for the new labels. It shouldn't bother her—being brushed off—but it did.

And Jet had kept his word to help Blaine each night. Leaving her to muddle through her evenings alone.

It left her feeling lonely. Unnecessary.

Maybe a tad taken for granted.

She shushed that thought. She had no right to expect anything from him or his family. They'd given her more than she could ask for, anyway. Who was she to want more?

Her phone rang. Morgan's name flashed on the screen.

"The store has a Now Hiring sign." Morgan's voice brimmed with excitement. "I have the number. Are you going to call?"

For all her thoughts about moving on, she should be thrilled at the news. But a slow drip of sadness went down to her gut. Calling about the job, getting an interview, getting hired, would permanently end this slice of her ideal life.

Mayer Canyon Ranch had provided her a cozy cottage to call her own. A job doing something she was passionate about. A family who treated her well, even if she wasn't and never would be one of them.

A man she couldn't stop thinking about.

"You haven't changed your mind, have you?"

"No, of course not." She forced her attention back to Morgan. "Let me get a pen and paper." She stretched forward, practically crushing Clara, to grab the small notepad and pen she kept on the coffee table. "Okay, I'm ready."

Morgan gave her the number. "You can move in with me anytime, you know."

"I appreciate it." She did, too. "But if they hire me, I should be able to find an apartment of my own before I'd have to start working."

"Well, make sure you aren't too far from me.

That way we won't have a long drive to swap kids for babysitting."

Babysitting. It left a sour, vinegar taste in her mouth. "Did you ever find the babysitter list you mentioned?"

"Oh, right." The sound of rustling came through. "Drake goes over to Cora's—she has a couple of kids of her own—on Mondays, Thursdays and Fridays. This other lady runs a day care out of her home. Her name's Rose. Drake goes there Tuesdays and Wednesdays. If I have to go in on Saturday, I usually get a high school girl to come over."

The schedule stabbed her brain, leaving her with a stress headache. It was bad enough thinking of Clara with one sitter—but three? She wanted her daughter to have a sense of normalcy.

Plus, she couldn't imagine worrying about three people potentially neglecting her baby.

"But when you get here, hopefully we can work out a better system between the two of us." Morgan sounded cheerful. "It will save us money, too. If you get hired, you'll work weekends, right?"

"Most likely."

"That solves at least one day for us right there."

She supposed it was true. It still didn't soothe her worries.

"I can't wait for you to meet Cameron. He's

taking me out tonight." Morgan described the outfit she bought for the date.

"Who will watch Drake?" Holly asked.

"My neighbor three doors down has a teen-age daughter. Don't get all overprotective on me. Drake's in good hands, and Clara will be, too. I'd better get ready. Let me know if you get an interview." They said their goodbyes and hung up.

Morgan made it sound easy. Was Holly just being overprotective?

She stared down at the baby, who'd fallen asleep. Then she looked at the paper in her hand.

If she didn't call the number, she'd regret it. Living here had always been temporary. And she'd be a fool to stay here indefinitely when her heart was already wrapped up so tightly with Jet, her job and the family.

The sooner she left, the sooner she could get over the Mayers.

Before they got over her for good.

She dialed the number.

Jet hadn't seen much of Holly in the past couple of weeks, and it was starting to eat away at him like the flesh-eating bacteria of a brown recluse spider's venom he'd seen on a television special not too long ago. He and Blaine had made a lot of progress at Grandpa's house. The new flooring was being installed this weekend, and the two of them had given every room a fresh coat of paint.

All the work had lit a fire under Jet to find his own house plan. He kept coming back to the same one in Randy's book. And he wanted to share it with Holly.

He pulled on his cowboy boots and reached for the handle of his front door. Paused before opening it. Rolled up Randy's book and slapped it against his thigh.

What could he say to her? He'd been avoiding her for days. Yeah, calving was still going strong, but he and Blaine and Jim and Mateo had it under control. They'd only lost one calf delivered stillborn, and there wasn't a thing they could have done about it.

The more he stayed away from Holly, the more he wanted to be with her.

She barely left the ranch that he could tell. It was Friday night. Maybe she'd want to go into town with him. Get some barbecue or something.

He opened the door, glad for the spring weather, tossed the book in the back seat of his truck, made his way across the lane and knocked on her door before he could talk himself out of it.

Ten seconds passed and he considered knocking again, but it opened to Holly with Clara on her hip. Her eyes widened. "Oh, it's you."

Not the welcome he'd been hoping for, but definitely the one he deserved. "Yeah, it's me. Have you eaten yet?"

She shook her head. She looked like she'd just woken from a nap. Her hair was tousled, eyes puffy.

"Want to go into town? Get some barbecue or something?"

"I don't think so." She kept her eyes downcast.

"Is something wrong? Are you not feeling well?"

"No, everything's fine. I'm fine."

"Well, you've got to eat, right?" He aimed for playful, but didn't quite nail it. More like desperate, to his ears. "I haven't seen you in a while and…" And what? What could he say? It was his own fault he hadn't seen her. He was the one who'd basically told her not to come over anymore. "I miss you."

Surprise lit her eyes. She stepped back. "Come in. I'll change."

Relief warred with guilt at her acceptance. "I'll take Clara for you."

"Okay."

As soon as the baby was in his arms, he realized how much he'd missed holding her.

Holly disappeared into the back of the cottage.

"Hey there, sweetheart," he said. Clara blinked up at him and smiled. He pointed to the sheep on her shirt. "What do we have here? Do you know what sheep say? Ba-a-a."

She stuck out her tongue, blowing bubbles and grabbing two fistfuls of his shirt. This kid made his heart pure mush. She smelled like baby shampoo and innocence. He caressed her fine hair, selected a board book from a pile on the floor and took her over to the couch. He got through five pages before she tried to yank it out of his hand.

"She's getting strong."

He hadn't realized Holly had returned. She stood off to the side, her head tilted, a thoughtful expression on her face.

He got to his feet, holding the baby. "She sure is."

Neither said anything for a few beats, but questions, apologies and something more lingered between them.

"Ready?" he asked.

She nodded, taking Clara from him and buckling her in the car seat. Soon the three of them were in his truck, driving on the main road as the sun lowered in the sky. They made small talk for the first ten minutes. She told him the new hire, Sadie, was catching on quickly and how wedding planning had taken over the office. He told her about Blaine's renovations and how many calves had been born.

Then it was if they ran out of things to say. Strange, really, since they never had before.

The restaurant was less than a mile out of town in the middle of the prairie. A parking lot full of cars showed the place was hopping. He found a spot and took the car seat out, carrying it to the entrance with Holly at his side. He itched to take her hand, to touch her, but it wasn't his place. This wasn't a date. No matter how much he wished it was.

They had to wait a few minutes before the waitress could seat them. Then they were tucked in a corner booth with Holly keeping Clara next to her. The baby sucked on a pacifier and seemed content.

He had to break the silence.

"I found—"

"I called—"

They had both spoken at once. Holly smiled and laughed, and he chuckled, too.

"You first." He hitched his chin to her.

"No, you. I insist." Her blue eyes shimmered.

He imagined they looked exactly like the ocean on a sunny day, not that he would know since he'd never been to the ocean. He still wanted to see it. Had been pushing thoughts of travel from his mind for so long, it almost surprised him how much he wanted to go. The desire to experience new places hadn't faded.

"I've been looking at house plans." Now why did admitting that make his hands all sweaty? "I think I found one."

"You did?" Her face lit up. "You'll have to show it to me sometime. I'd love to see it."

"Really? I have the book out in the truck."

"Why don't you get it?"

He didn't need to be told twice. "If a server comes around, would you order me an iced tea?"

She nodded.

Outside the sun dipped below the horizon with orange and pink and purple trailing behind it. He jogged to the truck, snatched the book and slowed his pace as he neared the entrance. He hadn't showed anyone the plan. Not Blaine, his usual confidant. Not his mom, who dragged everything out of him. Not the guys, either.

He wanted Holly to be the first. Because part of him wanted to share not only the plans with her, but the house, too, no matter how ludicrous the idea was.

Gulping, he went back inside, weaving through the tables and saying hi to people he knew until he reached the booth. He found the page and held the book open, handing it to Holly across the table.

A plastic glass with iced tea stood in front of him, and no sooner had he ripped the paper off the straw than the waitress arrived to take their order. They settled on burgers and fries. Jet angled his neck to check on Clara, asleep, sweet thing, then turned his attention to Holly as she studied the plan.

Did she like it? Hate it?

Did she even care about it?

About him?

Then her eyes met his. Shy eyes. And she sighed. A nice sigh.

"I feel like you snuck inside my head," she said. "This is exactly the house I would pick if I were you. Look at that big kitchen. And the front porch is so inviting. You're going to love it, Jet."

Hearing her approval chased all the nerves away. "I'm expanding to a three-car garage." He leaned over, pointing out details he was tweaking. To his surprise, she offered suggestions about the mudroom and kitchen pantry. They talked about the plan until their food arrived, at which point he closed the book and set it next to him in the booth.

"When do you think you'll break ground?" she asked, holding up a fry.

"I'm not sure." He squirted ketchup on his plate. "Probably this summer. Depends on when the contractor could start."

Her eyebrows drew together as her face fell.

"What?" he asked.

"Oh, it's nothing. I just realized I might not be around to see it."

He stopped chewing as he tried to make sense of her words. Then he choked down the French fry. "Why do you say that?"

"The store I worked for in Cheyenne is building one in Ogden. I called them, and they set up a phone interview for a week from today."

Ogden. Ogden…stupid Ogden. A burst of jealousy sparked through his chest. Not only would she be leaving Sunrise Bend, she'd be moving somewhere new, somewhere more exciting than here.

How could he compete with that?

"It's just an interview." She shrugged, gripping her burger. "I don't know if I'll get the job. They might not be willing to overlook the fact that I got fired from the other store."

She'd get it. He wasn't fool enough to hope she wouldn't. "When would you start?"

"No clue. The recruiter didn't say when they were opening."

"You know you can stay here, right?" He hoped he didn't sound desperate. "You fit right in. We all like having you and Clara around."

Her jaw tightened but she nodded. "I know."

He wanted to tell her she couldn't leave. Or try to convince her to stay. Or play on her fears about Clara to keep her around.

But he sank his teeth into the burger instead.

Holly wasn't his to hold on to. And he had to stop pretending she was.

Holly looked at the burger in her hand, but she'd lost her appetite. She fit right in? They liked having her and Clara around?

Jet probably thought he was saying all the right things, but he couldn't have said anything worse.

She didn't want to fit in or be around.

She wanted to be an important part of his life—their lives—integral, necessary. Here she'd thought he showed her the house plan because he was starting to feel something more for her. But for all she knew, he considered her a buddy or a sister, someone to bounce his plans off of, nothing more.

Oh, great, now her throat had a big old lump in it. Like she needed to be emotional at this moment.

A little voice in her head whispered, *Tell him you have feelings for him. Tell him the truth about Cody, how you fell in love with Jet before you even knew he existed.*

She couldn't do that! Setting the burger down, she tried to regroup. Revealing her feelings was a bad idea. What if he laughed? Or pitied her? Or went along with it even though he didn't feel the same?

No, she was keeping these feelings safe in her heart.

And if the interview went well, she was taking the job. She'd find a babysitter for Clara. She'd make it work. Because she couldn't stay here and keep feeling less than. It wasn't just Jet. It was Reagan and Julie. Constantly flitting from making the candles to the wedding plans and ignoring her.

She'd been down this road too many times. Until now, she'd put up with it, waiting for her mom or boyfriends to tell her they had no use for her anymore.

Not this time. She wasn't waiting around for the inevitable. She was better than that. If she got a job offer, she was taking it. No questions asked.

Chapter Eleven

She needed to talk to Jet.

On Thursday Holly watched out the cottage window for him to return. Dusk hadn't fallen yet, so she figured he'd be walking back soon. He'd stopped by a few times this week to see how she and Clara were doing. Each time she let him in, she'd had to grip her hands down by her sides and force herself to act normal. All she wanted to do was to tell him she loved him and wanted to stay. But he didn't have the same feelings. If he did, he'd want to spend more time with her.

How messed up was that? In love with her dead husband's brother.

She couldn't imagine it going over well with the rest of the family. It didn't even go over well with her most days.

But relief had arrived yesterday in the form of a formal job offer as the assistant manager of the bath and body shop in Ogden. She'd been hoping for a step up to manager, but they'd already promised the position to someone else. It was as good a job as she could hope for, so she'd accepted it.

The apartments she could afford in Ogden all had waiting lists, and she'd added her name to the list for one that would be available in a month's time. Until then, she'd move in with Morgan. Another thing she wasn't really looking forward to. As much as she loved her cousin, being crammed together with a toddler and baby would be stressful.

But, really, compared to where she'd been two months ago, what did she have to complain about?

Nothing. She should be filled with excitement over her new future. Too bad she wasn't.

A movement outside caught her attention. There he was, taking long strides to his cabin. She hurried to her front door and opened it, calling out, "Jet."

He turned when he saw her, immediately changing course to come over. "What's going on?"

"Can you come in for a minute?"

He nodded, a gleam in his eyes. When he looked at her like that, she wondered if maybe she was wrong and he did feel more for her than she believed. It couldn't come close to what she felt for him, though.

Her stomach felt like a punching bag. Maybe she should turn down the job. Stay here. She liked it here. She just didn't like being ignored.

It was probably wise to get to the point. "I got the job."

He blinked. His jaw shifted. And he lost some of the brightness he'd had a moment before.

"I see."

"I'll be the assistant manager." She turned, padding over to the couch and sitting. He followed her but remained standing.

"You took it?" He sounded hurt, surprised. She nodded. "What about my mom? My sister?"

"Sadie caught on quickly."

His eyes stormed. "Assistant manager...you should be the manager. Why don't you hold out for a better position?"

"They already hired one, and I feel blessed they're willing to take a chance on me at all."

"Don't take the job. You don't need it." He adopted a wide stance. "You have a job. Here."

Yeah, and she loved it. But she also loved him. And his family. And not having it reciprocated would slowly eat her alive. It already was.

"I'm moving Sunday."

"This Sunday?" His bellow echoed through the room. "But that's in a few days. No. No way."

She was taken aback. He didn't think he could forbid her, did he?

"Moving there isn't a good idea." He seemed... nervous. "You can't possibly have an apartment lined up. And if you do, you have no idea if it's in a good part of town or if you'll be in danger."

"I'm moving in with Morgan for the time being."

He began to pace, casting her a stern look. She'd never seen him like this. Like a grizzly bear on the prowl. "And who will watch Clara? You aren't the only one who cares about her, you know. We all love her and want her to grow up healthy and happy."

So did she. But his words rubbed the worry right back into her heart. She didn't have the babysitting situation figured out. Yet.

"That's why I'm moving now. It will give me a few weeks before my job starts to find someone I trust."

"The job doesn't even start for a few weeks and you're moving?" He looked dumbfounded. "No. It's not going to work, Holly. Stay here. You can work with Mom and Reagan, live here in the cottage, take care of Clara without needing a babysitter. I don't understand why you want to leave."

She didn't entirely, either.

"You need us," he said harshly. "You can't do it all on your own so far away."

Wait…what?

Holly felt like she'd been slapped. "Do you really believe that?"

He opened his mouth then shut it.

"I've been taking care of myself since I was seventeen years old, Jet. I don't need you." A fire lit in her core. "I *can* do it all on my own. I've done it for years."

He was shaking his head. She moved closer to him until inches separated them.

"You can't order me around. I'm not one of your responsibilities."

"That's where you're wrong."

Jet couldn't see straight, couldn't put a solid thought together if his life depended on it. She *was* one of his responsibilities. They all were. Every person, every animal, every employee on this ranch.

All.

His.

Responsibility.

"Jet, one of these days you're going to wake up and realize you aren't the master of this universe. All of your siblings are grown up. They're adults. They don't need you protecting them from whatever you think they need protection from. And I don't, either."

"You don't know." His voice scratched as his muscles tensed. "They need it."

"No, *you* need it." She backed up slightly. "That's why you put off dividing the ranch. It's not because you were too busy. You didn't think Blaine could handle it. And you made sure I worked with your mom and sisters because you thought they couldn't handle it without Erica. For all I know, you want me to work for them because you don't think I can handle any other job, either. Oh, Jet." Her face scrunched in disgust. "Your family isn't going to fall apart if you aren't here managing everything."

"You make me sound like I have some kind of hero complex." He didn't like the way he looked through her eyes.

"You do," she said as kindly as possible. "And it's ten times too big."

"You don't know anything." He stalked over to the front window then whipped back to face her. What did Holly know about being in charge of so much? He was the oldest, the one who'd always had to keep his siblings in line. His parents expected him to take charge. What else could he do? Dad had withdrawn over a year ago and was just now getting back to his old self. "I don't have a choice."

"A choice about what?"

"I *am* in charge. Ever since Dad unofficially retired, it's all on me. If something's wrong—with the ranch, one of the vehicles, the candle supplies, anything—I'm the first person they call. And I accepted that a long time ago. Someone has to be in charge. Someone has to make the sacrifices others aren't willing to make. I've been groomed for it since I was a small boy."

"I understand you have responsibilities here, Jet. I think you've let them consume you to the point you're afraid of anyone making a mistake." Holly dipped her chin. Then she met his gaze and her eyes pleaded with him. "It's condescending. Blaine can handle his half of the ranch. Your mom and Reagan can handle the candle business. I can handle moving to a new town."

He ground his teeth together. Condescending? She had no clue what she was talking about. Not one single clue.

"You know what would happen if you got on a plane and traveled to one of those places you told me about?" she asked quietly.

Yeah, he knew exactly what would happen. Some of the cattle wouldn't get checked and would wander off and die. Candle orders would get messed up, and Mom and Reagan would be devastated when the business collapsed. Blaine wouldn't know how to fix the tractor and chores wouldn't get done. They'd turn their backs on him. Blame him. Wouldn't talk to him.

They'd all run away like Cody had.

And he'd never see them again.

"Everyone would be just fine." Holly's voice cut through his horrible thoughts. He wanted to take her by the arms and make her promise just that. That everyone he loved would be just fine. That he could loosen his grip on all this. That he could have a life like his friends did. Hop on a plane and see parts of the world he'd always wanted to explore.

But he couldn't. Because he didn't believe her.

He didn't believe life turned out all right if you gave up control.

"You're wrong, Holly." He couldn't stand here and argue with her. He couldn't explain he was protecting the ones he loved. Including her. "Not everything turns out fine."

"Why don't you see yourself out?" Her words were low, clipped. "I have a lot of packing to do before I hit the road on Sunday."

He didn't bother responding. He was out the door in six long strides.

She'd see. She'd see she needed him—needed this ranch and this cottage and this job. And he wouldn't be the one who said *I told you so* when she came back.

* * *

After sleeping for only a few hours, Holly poured herself a cup of coffee in the showroom the next morning and waited for Julie and Reagan to arrive. Last week she'd told them about the job interview, so this shouldn't come as a big shock. If they reacted the way Jet had, though, she'd be heartbroken.

Like she wasn't already heartbroken.

She opened the fridge and poured cream into her mug, then stirred it mindlessly.

She'd fallen in love with a man who considered her helpless. Did he think she'd be unable to function if he wasn't providing a job and home for her and her baby?

Did his family feel the same?

Whatever reservations she'd had about leaving had vanished with his words.

The door to the showroom opened, and Julie and Reagan barely noticed her as they took off their coats and continued their discussion.

"I'll call the bakery about dessert for the bridal shower if you'll order the decorations," Julie said. "None of the stores around here have what I want, and neither of us has time to drive to the city."

"Oh, hi, Holly." A warm smile spread across Reagan's face. "You're here early." She walked over to Clara in the baby swing and played peek-a-boo for a moment.

"Can I talk to you both before the day starts?" Had an acid bomb detonated in her stomach? Her nerves were fried.

"What about?" Julie joined them.

"I got the job I told you about." The words landed like a thud.

Reagan's mouth opened in surprise, and Julie sucked in a loud breath.

"We thought you were happy here." Reagan sounded stricken.

Disappointment aged Julie. "Now, Reagan, that's neither here nor—"

"I've been very happy here." She gazed at Reagan then Julie. "I'm not leaving because I'm unhappy. This job has been fulfilling in every way—financially, creatively, personally."

"Then stay," Reagan pleaded.

Holly was tempted to. How could she not be? She got to do work she genuinely enjoyed, and she was able to spend every day with women she admired. Plus, there was the Clara factor. No need to hire a babysitter if she stayed.

But there was also the invisibility problem. The being-taken-for-granted problem. The not-really-being-part-of-the-family, no-matter-how-much-they-said-she-was, problem.

All of those could be overcome. She'd lived her

entire life not really belonging and being taken for granted.

What couldn't be overcome was the Jet problem. She'd fallen in love with someone who didn't love her or even respect her. He didn't think she was up to the task of managing her own life.

No, she could not stay.

"I can't." She tried to smile, but her lips wouldn't budge. "You knew I was planning to move to Utah. That never changed."

"Yes, but… I hoped you'd like it so much here, you'd stay." Reagan sighed. "What are we going to do without you?"

The words thawed the tundra around her heart. "Sadie is a quick learner. She practically knows everything already."

"Not designing the labels." Reagan shook her head, looking to the corner of the ceiling. "I'm sorry. I'm being selfish. I know you miss your cousin and have plans that don't include us. It's not like Sunrise Bend has so much going on."

It did, though. It had everything she needed. She'd never been one to go out much. She loved her little cottage. Loved this showroom. Loved the land, the mountains, the church, the town.

She wanted to reassure them, but the lump forming in her throat kept her silent.

"Reagan, why don't you turn on the equipment while I talk to Holly a minute?" Julie said.

When she was safely in the workshop, she turned to Holly. "We want you to stay."

Holly opened her mouth to speak, but Julie held up a finger.

"Hear me out," Julie said. "I—we—will respect your wishes. It took a lot of guts for you to start a completely new life here with a bunch of strangers. I'm sure there have been times, especially lately, when you've felt like the odd man out. We've all been preoccupied with Erica's wedding."

They had, but she understood. Kind of.

"I want you to know what a blessing you've been to us. You helped revamp our business. You gave us the direction we'd known we needed but had no idea how to pursue. Plus, you're easy to work with. You're a peacemaker, Holly, and the world needs those more than ever right now."

Tears threatened. How could she leave this woman who'd become such a mentor to her?

"But I have an inkling you're not leaving for your cousin or because you want to live in Utah, no matter how beautiful it is there." Julie stepped closer, taking both Holly's hands in hers. "I know my son."

Did she mean Cody? Holly froze.

"He's been lost since Cody died. More lost than the rest of us, but better at hiding it. And you've helped bring back my Jet. This is the first time I've seen him looking forward to the future rather than tolerating it. You're good for him. I don't know what's going on between you two, but whatever it is, it made a difference. You're already my daughter-in-law. You'll always be part of this family. But I'd be lying if I told you I haven't hoped you'd be more. With Jet."

Holly couldn't stop blinking. Those were the last words she'd ever expected to hear. And she didn't know how to respond.

"Don't say anything, hon," she said sadly. "I know Jet. Head made out of rock. You do what you have to do, but you're always—and I mean always—welcome here. The cottage is yours. The job is yours. Anytime. No matter what. Do you understand?"

Swallowing the emotion gripping her throat, she nodded. A tear slid out of the corner of her eye, and she wiped it away. Maybe she'd misjudged them. She hadn't realized Julie saw so much, but it didn't really surprise her.

"I hope I'm half as wise as you are someday, Julie."

Her smile lit her eyes with pleasure. "What a kind thing to say. No one has ever accused me of being wise. I guess there's a first time for everything."

Holly threw her arms around the woman and held on tightly. Julie patted her back.

"The Good Lord will work it all out, hon."

The words rang true, and she no longer had the acid-like nerves. *This I know, God is for me.*

"Always and forever."

"Amen."

Chapter Twelve

Sunday morning at the crack of dawn, Holly breathed in the cool air and said goodbye to each of the family members as Jet slammed her trunk shut. Erica and Blaine had passed Clara to Reagan, who couldn't hold back the tears dripping down her cheeks. After she said goodbye to Clara, Reagan passed her to Kevin and Julie, who said such elaborate goodbyes to the baby, it would have made Holly laugh if she wasn't so sad.

She was ripping their grandchild from them.

She hadn't realized it would hurt this much.

"Thank you," Holly said to Julie, "for everything you've done for Clara and me."

Julie hugged her tightly, whispering, "Remember what I said." Holly stepped back and nodded.

Then Kevin gave her an awkward pat on the

back. "You're a breath of fresh air. I'm proud my son chose you as his wife."

Her emotions couldn't take much more of this. She avoided looking at Jet. Last night she'd tossed and turned, wondering if she should address one of the elephants in the room. Kevin's words decided it for her. This family deserved to know her thoughts about Cody. They'd suffered because of his lies, and since moving here, she'd become convinced he would have opened up to her about them eventually.

"I know we don't talk about it, but I think you should know more about Cody." She paused to see how everyone was taking this and, at their obvious interest, she continued. "He was really happy when we met. He had a good job. He had plans for our life. We didn't know each other long, but we talked about buying a house someday and raising a family."

Julie exchanged glances with Kevin. They wrapped their arms around each other's waists, Kevin still holding Clara between them.

"I know finding out about me was a shock, and finding out he'd lied about you was even worse. But I think, in time, he would have told me about you. We would have come back here. You would have reconciled with him."

"Why do you think that?" Blaine's low voice

startled her. She met his gaze, her heart hurting at the despair in his eyes.

"Because you all love each other so much. You cared about him enough to force him to get his life together, and he did. I think he admired every one of you more than you'll ever know."

"How can you say that when he didn't even tell you about us?" Jet piped in.

"Because of the stories he told me about his childhood." She hadn't meant to tell them all. Not here. Not like this. Should she tell Jet privately?

"What do you mean?" Erica's eyebrows drew together.

Maybe it would be better for them all to know.

Holly held her head high. "He told me he saved a girl who fell through a hole in the ice. But since moving here, I found out Jet was the one who'd saved her. He also told me he saved his dog Buddy from a rattlesnake. Again, that was Jet. He claimed he was valedictorian. I think we all know who really held that title. He told me other things, too." Holly turned to Jet. "Everything he told me was a lie. About not having a family. About his heroic acts. He admired you, Jet. I think in some ways, he wanted to be you."

She turned to address everyone. "I think he felt ashamed of himself and was too embarrassed to come back. But in time, he would have. If he was strong enough to get his life together after leaving here, he would have been strong enough to reconnect with you, too."

Holly took Clara from Kevin. Her heart felt wrung out.

"Can I have a word with you?" Jet asked. "Alone?"

Everyone said one last goodbye, and then Julie waved the entire family to head back up the lane to the house. When they'd all gotten far enough away, Jet planted his feet, legs wide, and glowered at her.

Maybe she'd been wrong to tell him about Cody.

Maybe she'd been wrong all along.

"I can't believe you kept that from me." Jet reeled from what she'd revealed. Cody had told her he'd done the things Jet had done? Why would his little brother do that? Especially since Jet hated anyone talking about those things.

He never would have mentioned shooting the rattler the other day except being in that spot had sparked an emotional reaction to his fear of losing the dog. He wasn't heroic—he'd simply been in the right place at the right time.

"I pieced it together little by little." Holly stood tall, hoisting Clara higher on her hip.

"Why tell us now?" He stepped closer, his insides jumbled.

"We're all muddying through life after Cody, Jet. You. Your family. Me. I thought it might help you."

"Help me?" He moved even closer to her. "Nothing can help me. He's not coming back. I can't ever tell him how I feel. I can't tell him I'm proud of him for getting cleaned up and creating a good life for himself. I can't tell him how much I regret leaving things between us the way we did. I can't tell him he wasn't just a little brother to me. I felt more like his second dad. I protected him, disciplined him and believed in him. I really did believe in him, Holly, and he didn't know it. He'll never know it. I can't tell him how much I love him and miss him and wish he would have trusted us all more."

Where had that all come from? He averted his gaze, trying to calm his stampeding heartbeat.

"I think he knew." Her words were soft, comforting. Like her. "I'm mad, too, Jet."

"You? Why?" He could guess. He'd been rude to her, and he couldn't bring himself to apologize because he still wanted her to stay. He'd barely slept, worrying about what would happen when she got to Ogden.

"Because I married a man I thought I knew. But it turns out I married a stranger."

He stilled. He hadn't thought about how Cody's lies had affected her.

"I fell in love with the man Cody presented himself to be, but all he really did was present me with you." She tilted her head sympathetically. "And you are heroic. You are strong. Protective. A good brother. A good son. You'll make some woman a terrific husband. I… I care about you very much. But I won't fight for someone who thinks I'll fall apart without him."

He stood there speechless.

"Do me a favor, Jet." Her beautiful eyes shimmered. "Buy a plane ticket. Go somewhere. See the world. Your dad and Blaine will take care of the ranch. Nothing's going to fall apart without you."

He opened his mouth to give her all the reasons he couldn't, but she leaned forward and he forgot everything.

What was she doing? His body was paralyzed as she lifted up on her tiptoes and gently pressed her lips to his mouth. The touch was soft, rose-petal soft, and he ached to drag her into his arms and kiss her so hard she'd never dream of leaving him.

He wanted to tell her he'd protect her and Clara with his last breath. He'd provide for them, cherish them, move the mountains to the other side of the ranch for them. If only she'd stay.

But she'd already backed up.

"Life is short," she said with a wry frown.

"Cody taught us all that. You're a good man, Jet. Someday you're going to realize you deserve to be happy, too."

Then she opened the back door of her car, buckled Clara in her car seat and got into the driver's side. She paused a moment then hitched her chin to him.

And the door closed. The engine fired.

And she was gone.

Chapter Thirteen

Two weeks. It had been two of the longest weeks in Jet's life since Holly had left. He directed Rex over a gully and stared at the landscape before him. It was the middle of May already. Summer would be here soon. Wildflowers were bursting through the earth. Everything was being renewed…even him.

He'd changed.

Holly had changed him.

After she'd left, he'd gone back to his cabin and sat there in a numb trance for hours. Then something had broken inside him. He'd cried. Bawled, really, until all his guilt and rage and sorrow over Cody's death dissipated.

He hadn't known he needed to grieve. Hadn't even known he'd been putting off grieving until Holly had told them Cody would have reconciled with them. That night, Jet finally believed her. Because he'd prayed.

He'd begged God for forgiveness for all the ways he let Cody down, and he thanked God for being with his brother when the family cut him loose. He also thanked God for sending Holly to his brother. And he realized how wrong he'd been to skate by all year telling himself he'd been doing the right thing when all he'd been doing was holding on to everyone too tightly instead of relying on the Lord.

Later, his mom had stopped by, and for the first time since he was a boy, he'd let her hold him. They'd sat on his couch, with him in her arms, rocking him like she had when he was a child. He'd needed that, too.

"You're going to be all right, Jet." She'd taken her finger and swept the hair at his forehead. "This has been hard on you."

He'd wanted to ask which part—losing Cody, watching Dad withdraw, or losing Holly and Clara? But he'd been too chicken to ask. And looking in her big, compassionate eyes, he figured she knew it all anyhow. She didn't miss much, his mom.

After she left, he'd asked God for the light yoke only He could give. From now on, he wanted to be in step with Jesus.

The next day he'd called a local handyman and

had him estimate the cost and timeline of fixing up all the outbuildings on Blaine's property. He and his brother had even created a schedule for when each phase of splitting the ranch needed to happen to meet their goal date of September first.

He took in a deep breath, admiring the view but wishing Holly was there to share it with him.

Last weekend, he'd gotten the nerve to call her. To his surprise, she'd answered. He told her about his and Blaine's plans for the ranch. She, in turn, told him the apartment she wanted was going to be available a week early, which left less than a month of her living with her cousin. All the things he wanted to say—needed to say— about how much he admired her, how he was a fool to make her think she couldn't make it on her own, how desperate he'd been to get her to stay—remained shriveled up inside him. He'd been too scared to let them out.

He also hadn't mentioned love. It was enough to hear her voice.

So he'd called her the next night. And the next. And he would until she told him not to. Because he needed her in his life even if she was in Utah.

And the past two weeks had made him realize something else. No one really needed him that much. Not his brother, not his sisters, not his mom, not his dad.

Holly had been right all along. They were capable adults. They got along fine without him being in charge.

Turning the horse around, he guided it back through the pasture, past the stable, across the lane toward his property. He hadn't contacted Randy's builder yet. The house plan book still sat in the back of his truck, where he'd left it since the night he'd taken Holly out for burgers.

Sunshine mingled with the cool air. Everyone in his family was moving on. Erica would be married in three weeks. Reagan and Mom had authorized Sadie to hire another part-time employee. Blaine had gone on a shopping spree to fill Grandpa's house with new furniture. Even his parents were planning a trip to visit Holly and Clara next month after the wedding hoopla was over. He still didn't know if Holly was coming to Erica's wedding. It depended on if she could get off work or not.

Where did that leave him?

When he reached the spot where he planned on breaking ground, he dismounted Rex. A truck pulled into the long drive and turned down the dirt lane toward him before coming to a stop not far from where he stood.

Randy hopped out and strode over to him, grinning. "This is it, huh?"

"What?"

"Where you're building." He looked at the site,

nodding and smiling. "I figured I'd find you here. Did you pick out your plan?"

Jet ducked his head. He'd been so excited about the house before blowing it with Holly. He hadn't even told her the truth—that he loved her. What kind of coward was he?

"I did, but I'm putting it on hold for now." He swallowed, trying to sound firm.

"Why?" Randy poked around the site, pausing at the exact spot where Jet pictured the front porch. "Blaine told me you two have a solid plan to divide the ranch. Calving's about done. I figured you'd be jumping on it."

"I was, but it doesn't seem important at the moment."

"I'm not following." Randy sounded as clueless as he looked, and he was usually a smart guy.

"Why build a big house for one person?" He kicked at a clump of green needlegrass. "The cabin suits me fine."

"Well, I'm building a big house, and I'll be the only one living in it." Randy gestured behind him. "What's wrong with that?"

"Nothing." There wasn't anything wrong with it. He didn't know what to say. "I mean maybe you'll have a family someday."

"No, that will *not* happen." He sounded so resolute Jet was taken aback. Randy had always been adamant about not marrying. Then again, they'd all said they weren't the marrying kind. But Jet wasn't feeling so anti-marriage anymore. "I'm building this house for me."

Jet stared at him through new eyes.

"Look, man," Randy said. "I don't know what's going on with you, so if I'm out of line, tell me to shut up and I gladly will."

Huh.

"Late last year I was sitting in church, nodding off during the sermon."

Jet's lips twitched with amusement. He could relate.

"And I heard the pastor say something that changed my life."

"What?"

"He quoted from the Bible. I don't recall the exact book or verse, but basically he said, 'I came that they may have life and have it abundantly.' The words rolled around in my head, waking me up for good. I realized right then and there I'd been putting off my dreams. If the Bible says Jesus came so I could have an abundant life, why wasn't I doing anything about it? I called Larry at Jackson Realtors the next day to find me land."

"I didn't know building a house was one of your dreams."

"I didn't, either. But I did know I wanted property I could fish on, and I also knew living with Austin had grown stifling. I love him, but we're both pretty stubborn. I was ready for my own place."

Jet took in Randy, so confident and hopeful, and he wanted what he had. He wanted an abundant life, too.

"You should come out and see the house. It's framed. The windows and doors are in. It's really coming along."

"I'll do that." Jet cocked his head to the side. "You busy? Come back to the cabin. I'll show you the plan I picked out."

Randy grinned. "I'll meet you over there."

Five minutes later, Jet sat across from Randy at his table, pointing out the details of the house plan. Randy asked questions, gave him tips about materials and finally glanced up with approval.

"Call my builder. He does a good job." Randy stood. "I've got to go. Text me when you want to stop by the construction site."

"I will." He walked Randy to the door and said goodbye. Then he returned to his living room and sank into his couch.

Maybe Randy was onto something. Jet had finally loosened his grip on managing his family members, but in the process, he felt lost. Useless.

Undeserving.

He'd put the house on hold because he couldn't see himself in it without Holly and Clara. Was he putting his life on hold, too? His dreams?

Holly's gentle voice echoed in his mind. *Buy a plane ticket...*

He wasn't quite ready to do that. Not with pregnant stragglers who hadn't had their calves yet. Not to mention, the upcoming wedding and...

There it was. Her voice again. *Someday you're going to realize you deserve to be happy, too.*

Sounded an awful lot like Randy's revelation. All these voices were messing with him. He couldn't just buy a plane ticket. Everyone else's happiness came before his, and who was he to live an abundant life?

God, I'm really messed up. I know Holly's right. I stifled my brother, didn't give my mom and sisters enough credit, and I told Holly straight-out she couldn't handle it on her own in Utah. I was wrong. About everything.

His chest burned with humiliation.

And worse, she didn't even know why he'd done it. He hadn't even known why until recently. He felt responsible for not preventing Cody's involvement with substance abuse. After his death, he'd tried to cushion everyone else around him—keep them close—so he wouldn't have to worry about history repeating itself.

But he'd only ended up stifling them. Making them resent him. And, in the process, ended up looking like a fool.

He wanted to feel like Randy, taking charge of his life and making his dreams come true. But it wasn't the house that would fulfill him—it was who would be with him in the house.

God, I don't know what to do. Should I go ahead and build even though every empty room will remind me Holly should be here? And it's only been two weeks, but she texted me a picture of Clara yesterday, and I can't believe how big she's gotten. I'm already missing too much of the baby's life. I don't know what to do.

His frustration begged to be released.

Spending time with Holly had been a privilege. She was the one who'd listened to his day, been interested in his life, asked him what he wanted, helped him see what he needed.

She cared. And he'd been drawn to her not because his warped mind told him she needed him. No, he'd welcomed spending time with her because she made him feel less lonely. She took some of the burdens off his shoulders.

Just being with her made him feel approved.

Holly had that way about her, and he missed it more than he ever thought possible.

He loved her.

He loved her so much. He didn't know how or why, but every day that went by, he loved her even more.

Sighing, he stood. It didn't matter how he

felt. She had a new life in Utah, one she seemed happy with.

And no matter what happened, he had a life here in Sunrise Bend he'd never turn his back on. Maybe it was time to take a step in the direction of an abundant life. He thought about his land, the house plans, the future.

God, thinking about building a house—doing anything I want, really—makes me uncomfortable.

Was his reluctance about Holly? Cody? What?

He didn't want to make a mistake. But he had a feeling he was going to be okay.

It was time to move on. God would be with him, no matter what.

"When will you be back?" Holly followed Morgan to the front door of the apartment.

"I'm not sure. Not late, don't worry." Morgan turned back to her, gave her a quick hug and reached for the door handle. "Thanks for watching Drake for me. It's so great having you here."

Morgan slipped out into the waning sunshine. Holly gave a half-hearted wave to Cameron, who waited for Morgan on the sidewalk.

Life in Ogden was exhausting compared to life in Sunrise Bend.

It was the third night this week she'd been left with Drake so Morgan could go on a date.

And she was already babysitting him during the days when Morgan worked. The first week she'd been here, it hadn't bothered her. But they'd just wrapped up week two, and Holly was getting tired of spending all day and most of the evening with a baby and toddler all by her lonesome.

Backtracking to the living room, she picked up toys and tossed them into an empty hamper as Drake ran in circles waving his hands over his head, shouting at the top of his lungs.

"Please stop shouting, Drake." The child paused then resumed running and yelling. "Drake!" She hated raising her voice, but with her temples throbbing and another long night ahead of her, it couldn't be helped.

"Aunt Howee?" His little face fell and he ran up to her, throwing his arms around her legs. "Pway bus, Aunt Howee." Then he bounced up and down, his head back as he looked up at her. "Pwease? Bus?"

She rallied every ounce of patience left in her body and picked the boy up. She hugged him before he squirmed to be let down. It wasn't his fault Morgan was in the early throes of love. And, honestly, Holly didn't fault her cousin for it. Morgan had been so encouraging ever since she'd arrived.

She'd taken Holly on a tour around the city, introduced her to her friends and gone shopping for new baby clothes for Clara. Morgan deserved some happiness.

"No bus right now, Drake. Aunt Holly needs to rest. Let's watch a cartoon." She hated plopping him in front of the television, but she had nothing left to give today. "I'll watch it with you."

They went to the couch. As Drake climbed onto her lap, he kept asking her to play bus. If her head wasn't aching, she would indulge him. The simple game made him so happy. She'd set him on her lap and pretend they were driving a bus together. It would go fast. It would go slow. Sometimes it would stop quickly with a screech. And he loved every second of it.

Clara was still asleep in the portable crib in Drake's bedroom, thankfully. How the child slept through his shouting was a mystery she hoped never got solved. At least she'd have her own place soon. A few more weeks.

Felt like an eternity at this rate.

She clicked the remote and found a cartoon. Drake nestled his dark curls against her chest. It was times like this she adored the energetic toddler. But when he threw toys and got rough with Clara and refused to listen to Holly…well, those times weren't so great. And they happened often. At least it was preparing her for when Clara hit the terrible twos.

How she missed her cottage on Mayer Canyon

Ranch. She missed her job. Missed Reagan and Julie and designing the labels.

Most of all, though, she missed Jet.

Her love for him hadn't faded. The first time he'd called—a week ago or so—her heart had practically pitter-pattered right out of her chest. And then he'd called again. And again. Until it became a nightly routine.

At first she thought maybe he was checking up on her, confirming to himself she'd made a mistake and couldn't handle life away from them. But she hadn't detected even a hint of condescension or anything. She got the impression he was calling because he genuinely wanted to talk to her.

That made two of them. She genuinely wanted to talk to him, too.

Drake, bless his heart, stopped begging to play and let out a big yawn. He twisted his neck to look up at her. "I wike George monkey."

"I do, too, sweetie." She watched as Curious George held hands with the man in the yellow hat. As Drake's body relaxed against hers, her headache eased.

Was this—Ogden—what she really wanted?

She'd called two babysitters, toured three home day cares and felt better about her options for Clara on the days Morgan wouldn't be able to watch her. Holly was set to start work next

Wednesday. She should be excited to start her new life.

But she wasn't. Not at all.

In fact, the innermost part of her kept whispering she'd made a mistake.

Moving here had been a mistake.

But why?

It all added up to the right choice. Didn't it?

In Ogden she wasn't at the mercy of the Mayer family's generosity. She didn't feel invisible or indebted or like she was a responsibility they'd absorbed. No, here she called the shots. Here, she...

Wasn't part of a team that valued her ideas.

Didn't have her own space...yet.

Didn't have much of a support system. Morgan had a big heart but was as time-crunched and money-strapped as Holly.

Holding Drake, an unwelcome thought occurred. Had her move here been a different kind of rash decision than the ones she'd made with her exes? A way of avoiding the truth that Cody's death and the introduction of his family had kicked up?

In the past she'd made a habit out of clinging to anyone who showed interest in her. She'd believe the promises they'd made her, no matter how empty. And she'd gotten burned again and again.

Inhaling sharply, an ugly realization took hold. She hadn't left Mayer Canyon Ranch because

of Jet. Or because his family had been preoccupied and hadn't been paying her much attention. And it wasn't because she'd been dying to
live in Utah.

She'd left because she'd been scared.

Terrified Jet was the real deal.

And if he was the real deal, eventually he'd
see she wasn't worth loving, just like everyone
else had.

But what if she'd been wrong all this time?
She'd blamed herself for every relationship that
had gone bad, and yes, she'd glommed on to
the wrong guys. So desperate to not be alone,
to have someone care about her, she'd accepted
any smooth talker who looked her way.

But Jet wasn't like them.

They'd been all talk.

He was all action.

She shifted slightly. Drake must have been exhausted. He'd fallen asleep, and his soft snores
made her rest her chin on the top of his head.
Poor little guy. So much energy. Maybe he'd
needed her to cuddle him so he could relax.

And maybe Jet needed something similar
from her. He wasn't the relaxed type. Bore the
weight of the ranch and his family on his shoulders 24/7, whether they needed him to or not.
But when Holly was with him, he relaxed, let
his guard down.

Like when he'd showed her his house plans. She'd loved the excitement in his tone, the way he'd allowed himself to hope, to think about his own needs for a change. He'd stopped by her cottage night after night, showed her the spot where he was building his house, and even now, he continued to call her.

Why was she so certain Jet would tire of her? Why did she keep defaulting to *I'm not worth loving* mode?

Sure, her dad had abandoned her, and her mom wasn't much better. But Morgan had stuck by her all these years. And Kevin and Julie were already making plans to come out to see her and Clara. Erica kept texting her to come to the wedding. Reagan had called several times to chat about the candles. Not everyone turned their backs on her. Least of all Jet.

Did she really, truly, believe the Bible passage she'd kept so dear to her heart? Did she believe *This I know, God is for me*?

When it came down to it, she'd known Jet had been lying to her when he'd claimed she couldn't make it out here on her own. She'd also known he'd been lying to himself. For whatever reason, he was clinging to a fantasy he was somehow responsible for the happiness and well-being of his entire family.

Julie's comment about how Cody's death had

affected Jet more than he'd let on had touched her deeply.

That overinflated sense of duty. Hmm…he wouldn't have tried to stop her if he hadn't cared about her the way he did the rest of his family.

She sighed. What did it matter? She was here in Utah, and he was there in Wyoming.

She could analyze it up and down, but what good would it do?

She couldn't change what had happened. Even so, she was sure glad he called every night.

Chapter Fourteen

Saturday after the ranch chores were finished, Jet stopped by Blaine's house. Waiting on the front porch, he took in the immediate area. Blaine must have tackled the landscaping. The bushes were trimmed, and a new welcome mat greeted him. The entrance was fresh and inviting. White and purple wildflowers bloomed across the plains in the distance.

Jet was ready for his own life to bloom. Starting today.

"What's up?" Blaine let him inside. They made their way to the kitchen, where Jet took out a stool and sat.

"I need a favor."

"You? A favor from me?" He pointed to Jet then back to his own chest.

"Yes." Jet rolled his eyes. "Don't act so shocked."

"I'm all ears." Blaine grinned.

"I'm taking off for a week."

"Taking off? Like not working or—"

"I'm going on a road trip."

"Where?"

"I dunno yet. I just need to shake things up."

"It's about time." Blaine smiled, working a knot out of his left shoulder. "You've always wanted to travel."

"I'll talk to Dad. See if he'll come out and help this week."

"He will." Blaine seemed sure of it. "Ever since Holly and Clara came into our lives, he's been more himself."

"Yeah, I noticed it, too." The heavy sadness that had stolen Dad's words and drive had melted with the last snows. More often than not, his father had the old sparkle in his eyes. He wanted to stay retired, though, and Jet couldn't blame him for that. He'd worked hard his entire life. He deserved to rest.

"Maybe you should head to Utah on that road trip." Blaine grew serious. "See how Holly and Clara are doing."

He'd been thinking the same thing. "I don't want her thinking I'm checking up on her."

"Look, I know you. Until she came along, you were barking out orders and as hard to be around as Dad."

Jet squirmed. He was?

"But having Holly here…well, she made you human again. She's good for you. I think she likes you. I know you like her."

"She was Cody's," he said gruffly.

"Yeah, she was," Blaine said, averting his gaze. "It's hard. Hard knowing he's gone."

Jet couldn't argue with that.

"But life goes on. For the ranch. For us. For her." He hesitated. "Look, I know we all said we weren't getting married. Don't expect me to change my mind anytime soon. But it doesn't mean you can't change yours."

"Why do I feel like you're a lot smarter than I ever gave you credit for?" Jet gave him a sideways glance.

"Because I am." Blaine grinned.

"Okay, okay, I'll think about it." He jerked his thumb behind him. "I'm going home to pack. I'll stop by and talk to Dad before I leave. You need anything, call me."

"Come here." To Jet's surprise, Blaine pulled him in for a quick hug. "Thanks for all your help here. And thanks for working with me to get my half of the ranch in shape. It's nice—real nice—to feel like you trust me."

"I've always trusted you."

"No, you haven't." He shrugged. "It's okay. You do now."

"Hey, man, that's on me. I…" He sighed. "I

didn't really trust myself. I think I was holding on too tightly. Because of Cody."

Understanding weaved between them. Then Jet nodded and turned to leave. "Like I said—"

"I'll call if I need anything." He followed him to the door. "Have fun. And go straight to Utah."

"Ha, ha." Not looking back, Jet raised his hand in goodbye and left.

The next morning at dawn, he was rumbling down the long lane away from Mayer Canyon Ranch. Last night he'd loaded the truck, talked to his dad—who assured him he'd be glad to work the ranch all week with Blaine—and avoided his mom and sisters. He didn't need their input on where he should go. He already knew exactly what they'd say anyhow.

A sense of anticipation had him drumming his thumbs on the steering wheel.

This was it. He was finally getting away. Not on an errand. Not for work. Not for his family.

For an adventure.

His itinerary blazed through his brain. Head north to Billings, Montana, then drive to Yellowstone, hike around Mammoth Hot Springs, stay the night, then tomorrow drive west to Idaho and continue south until…

Utah.

It was the longest route, but it would allow him to see four states instead of two. And now that he was finally on the road, he wanted to see them all.

The hours passed quickly and, after a pit stop in Billings, he cast a longing eye toward Beartooth Highway. Still closed for the season. How he would have liked to drive along the highest-elevation paved highway in the northern Rocky Mountains. He'd heard it was spectacular with over twenty mountain peaks.

Next time.

And there would be a next time. He was sure of it.

He passed magnificent views under blue skies until he reached Gardiner and turned into the north entrance to Yellowstone. He kept the truck to a crawl as he craned his neck to see everything around him—mountains, boardwalks, trees. Soon he'd parked at the lower level and joined the other hikers on the boardwalk.

A hill-like terraced rock formation in colorful hues greeted him. White blended with coppery orange then faded to gray and yellow. It was stunning. He stood there taking it in for a few minutes before continuing on. Next he studied Mound Terrace, steam rising above the block-like rock formations as a trickle of clear water revealed algae below.

Walking up the stairs to Upper Terrace Drive, he couldn't help marveling at the natural beauty of it all. And he wished he had someone there to share it with.

Not his brother. Not his parents. Not his sisters. Not his friends.

He wanted to share it with Holly. To point out the various springs along the way. She would love it here.

As he continued, he noted the rich colors of Grassy Spring and the desolate, almost tundra-like aspect of this section of the hike. Then he reached Canary Spring and stood there, awed by the brilliant turquoise of the water against the white sediment. Steam wreathed above it.

Holly had unlocked the part of him he hadn't allowed out in a long time. He was here because of her.

And he didn't want to be here without her. In fact, he didn't want to spend another minute without her.

Forget the itinerary. Forget the sightseeing. From this moment forward he was on a one-way nonstop road trip to Ogden, Utah.

Breaking into a jog, he hauled back to the truck, got in and started the engine.

Holly was right. Life was short. And he wanted her in his.

She missed her life with the Mayers. Holly pushed the stroller along the sidewalk. She still hadn't had her first day of work. On Tuesday she'd gotten a call from her new boss that the opening was delayed until the first week of June. She thought she'd be more disappointed. But each day that passed, she found herself not wanting the job at all.

She didn't want to live here.

The love she felt for Jet wasn't going away. He still called her every night. He gave her updates on the family and the cattle, and she told him Clara's latest milestones as well as the parks she'd found for the kids. It turned out Drake loved the outdoors. Morgan had joined them on one of her days off this week, too. It was nice. But not as nice as Wyoming.

It had taken being away from Sunrise Bend for her to get her head on straight. Before she'd met the Mayers, she'd buried her questions about Cody's family. Then, after she'd gotten to know them, when she'd realized he'd lied to her about his past, she'd felt betrayed and hurt and confused.

She was finally ready to forgive Cody. She'd fallen for a rash, fun-loving man who treated her like she was special. But he'd also been too afraid to reveal his true self to her, and that's why he'd lied.

He'd probably thought she'd reject the real him, the one who'd disappointed his family and hadn't been a hero. They hadn't known each other well enough to trust each other.

Lord, I have so many mixed feelings about Cody, but none of them matter anymore. I just want to thank You for bringing him into my life. Thank You for blessing me with Clara. And thank You for introducing me to Cody's family. Especially Jet.

For the first time in her life, she was in love— a real, mature, lasting love.

The green grass and fresh leaves on the trees made everything appear shiny and new. Her heart felt shiny and new, too.

As hard as it was, she'd been coming to a decision all week.

She didn't want to live in Ogden.

She wanted to move back to Sunrise Bend. To get her job back with Mayer Canyon Candles. But only if Jet could see a future with her and Clara in it.

That was the part jangling her nerves.

He liked her—she knew he did—but was it enough?

Holly stumbled and gripped the stroller handle tightly. She'd never pursued a guy before. Never been the first to tell him how she felt, either. But this year had changed her. Made her stronger.

She was ready to take a chance. She was going to tell Jet she loved him. And if he felt the same, she was going to suggest moving back to Sunrise Bend. Of course, she'd have to talk to Julie and Reagan about also getting her job back. Hopefully, they hadn't been lying when they'd said she'd always be welcome there.

She missed them all so much.

Of course, this would mean breaking the news to Morgan. And canceling the apartment. And telling her new boss to hire someone else. All three of those things made her nauseous. But they would be worth it.

At least, they would if Jet loved her, too.

What if he didn't, though? A park bench ahead beckoned. She rolled the stroller next to it and sat. Clara reached her hands up, bunching her little fingers for Holly to lift her out of the stroller. Holly set her on her lap, facing her.

"What do you think, peaches? You miss Grammy and Grandpa?"

Clara smiled, gurgling, reaching for her hair and yanking it.

"Ouch. You don't want me to go bald, do you?"

Jet was the one who'd lent her a helping hand when she'd needed it the most. He cared about everyone around him. He'd sacrificed time and again for her, for his family, even for the cows and calves.

She'd never met anyone like him, and she never would because he was one of a kind. It was time to cloak herself in courage, because tonight when he called, she was going to tell him how she felt.

She just prayed he loved her, too. Because life outside of Sunrise Bend didn't excite her at all.

Jet pulled into a gas station in Ogden as his cell phone rang.

Mom.

Tentacles of panic spread through his veins. Was something wrong at the ranch? He ticked through the options—Dad, Blaine, Reagan, Erica. Anything could have happened to them.

Take a deep breath. Stupid to get so worked up. No matter how much he tried, he'd never shake the memory of the call from the police that his brother had been in a car accident and hadn't survived. He'd been listed as Cody's emergency contact. Jet would be forever grateful he'd been the one to break the news to his parents rather than the officer.

"Hey, Mom, what's going on?" He was surprised his voice sounded so steady.

"Just checking in." Her cheery voice chased all his fears away. "How was day one of your road trip?"

"Good. I went to Yellowstone."

"Oh, how nice. I remember going there with your dad when you were a little boy..." She continued to prattle on about a trip he had no memory of.

As much as he wanted to cut her off and speed to Holly's, he didn't. He listened and answered her questions.

"Where are you off to next?" Her voice sounded small.

Was she worried about him? He hadn't thought anyone worried about him anymore.

"I'm going to Holly's. I have some things I need to say."

"Oh?" It came out high, unnatural, like a melody skipping an octave.

"Yeah. I'll call you tomorrow and let you know how it goes."

"Oh, good. You're doing the right thing. I'm glad you're there. She's good for you. For all of us. I miss her and the baby so much."

"I know you do. I do, too, Ma. I'm not here for a friendly visit. I… I have feelings for her."

"I know you do."

"You do?" How did his mother always seem to know so much?

"I won't keep you. You be sure to call me. First thing tomorrow. Or later tonight. Anytime at all, hon."

"Tomorrow." He loved her, but she was pushing it.

"How about a little text? Just so I know?"

"Ma…"

"All right, all right." There was that exasperated tone he was used to. "I'll say a prayer."

"Thanks, Mom. I love you."

"I love you, too."

He hung up before he got any mushier. What was the matter with him? Leaving the ranch. Driving to Yellowstone. Coming to Ogden. Confiding in his mother?

He grinned. He was in love. That's what was going on. And if he wasn't so scared, he'd be telling everyone how he felt.

He checked the time. Going on seven. Exactly when he typically called Holly.

He'd be talking to her at seven tonight. Except this time he'd be talking to her face-to-face.

He couldn't wait.

Chapter Fifteen

❧

Holly slid the patio door open and went onto the balcony to wait for Jet's call. Morgan was inside with the kids, and Cameron had stopped by, too. He was roughhousing with Drake, who kept shrieking and running back for more. Holly smiled and took a seat. Cameron was good for Morgan and Drake. She hoped they'd stay together.

When five minutes passed, she began pacing the balcony. It was Sunday night. Did Jet have plans? Maybe he'd gone to Mac's. Or Blaine's.

Or maybe he didn't want to continue their nightly conversations. Her heart thumped. That couldn't be it.

Why wasn't he calling?

Maybe she should call him.

And say what?

The swish of the sliding door made her turn.

Jet?

He was here!

In two steps, she was in his arms, and it felt so right, she could barely breathe. She clung to him.

He stepped away first, gazing into her eyes.

"You're here," she said.

"I'm here." His eyes shimmered with pleasure. "Is there anywhere we can go that's more private?" He hitched his thumb behind her where Drake's face and hands were pressed against the glass, and Morgan and Cameron were watching them with way too much interest. Morgan grinned as she held Clara and made her wave her little arm to them. Holly groaned, grabbed Jet's hand, slid open the patio door and led him into the living room.

"Morgan, Cameron, this is Jet Mayer. Jet, this is Morgan and Cameron. We're leaving." Still holding his hand, she didn't stop walking until they were out the front door.

As soon as it shut behind them, she turned to him, and his chest was right there. Her hands curled into his Western shirt to steady herself. She looked up into those brown eyes she'd missed so much.

He made a growling sound and pulled her close, pressing his mouth to hers. His kiss was like a wax seal over her heart. A claim. A promise. And she wound her arms around his neck, urging him closer, pouring all her pent-up feelings for him into the kiss.

"Come on," he said, finally pulling back slightly, "let's go someplace we can talk."

He tenderly ran his fingers down the hair edging her face, and she brushed her lips against his again.

"Holly." The word was a plea.

"There's a gazebo behind the building."

He took her by the hand, neither of them speaking as they strolled down the sidewalk to the pretty, white gazebo. It was still daylight out, though the sun was falling lower in the sky. When they stepped into the gazebo, Holly let go of his hand and leaned against the railing, facing him.

"It's so good to see you." He shook his head in amazement. "Since you left, I've learned a lot."

"I have, too."

His jaw kept clenching, and she watched in fascination as the muscle flexed in his cheek. "I realized I'm overbearing. Selfish. Way too overprotective. And not too smart."

She frowned. Those were the last words she ever thought she'd hear him say. "Excuse me?"

He nodded, taking off his cowboy hat and running his hands through his hair. He set the hat on the bench. "It's all true. I couldn't see what an uptight bore I'd become after Cody died."

"I never thought of you as a bore." Where was all this coming from?

"That's because you're nice, Holly. You see the best in people. You bring out the best in people."

Oh. She wanted to fan herself.

"My baby brother was the most blessed guy on the planet for marrying you. And I stupidly treated you like you were a three-year-old trying to ride a bike without training wheels. I'm sorry, Holly. I said a lot of dumb stuff when you told me you were moving."

"Yeah, well, change is hard for you."

"It is, but don't make excuses. You were right. About all of it. I was stifling my family. Condescending. Holding them back. And for what? They are all capable, amazing people. I'm surprised they put up with me this long."

"Oh, Jet." All she wanted to do was to hold him and to tell him to stop beating himself up, but she remained rooted in place.

"Not done." He held up a finger. "I've never gone a day in my life without having family to rely on. I took it for granted. I didn't realize what a blessing they are to me until I met you and saw how hard life was for you when we first met. Holly, I don't know how you did it. You were taking care of the baby, sick, unemployed—and yet you were still determined to protect Clara and make life work. You must have steel in your blood. You're one of the strongest people I've ever met."

A knot tied in her throat, and she couldn't speak if she wanted to. She couldn't believe he'd said all that.

"No matter what happens in my life, I've got a safety net to fall back on. My family." His stance softened as his voice lowered. "And you didn't. I was disrespectful to claim you needed me and the ranch or you'd fall apart. You don't need me. You don't need the ranch. You're not going to fall apart. You've got guts."

That's where he was wrong. She needed him. She needed the ranch. She needed it all desperately.

"But, Holly, here's the thing." He took a step closer to her. "I need you. You listen to me, and I feel safe telling you my dreams, simple as they are. I like talking to you about my day. Sharing a meal with you. You soften my rough edges, and we both know there are a lot of rough edges."

A tear slipped from of the corner of her eye, and she wanted to laugh, to cry, to tell him everything in her heart, too.

Jet gave her a sheepish look. "When I loosened my iron grip on everyone, I was finally able to grieve Cody's death. I didn't even know I needed to."

"I'm glad. I'm sorry, but I'm glad." It must

have been so hard for him. She wished she could have been there to help him through it.

"And without me trying to control my brother and sisters, everyone's breathing easier. The ranch is fine. Blaine's doing great. The candle business is better than ever. Erica's wedding is on track. Everyone's fine. Everyone but me."

She blinked, wiping away another tear.

"I love you, Holly. I know you were my brother's to have and to hold till death do you part, but I can't keep pretending I don't want you for myself. So, if you're not over Cody, tell me and I'll accept it. But if you have a little bit of feelings for me—"

"I love you, too." She knew she had the deer-in-headlights look, and she didn't care. He'd shared his deepest thoughts with her. It was her turn to do the same. "I think I loved you before I even met you. You're wrong about no one needing you. You're the rock your family leans on, Jet. I lean on you, too. It's incredible, really, to have someone so solid to rely on."

He opened his mouth, but she shook her head. "I'm not done, either. I haven't always had the best taste in men. When I met you, I was lost. Confused. As desperate as I've ever been. But you treated me with kindness, as if I mattered. And you were patient, understanding, especially about Clara. You took me in, gave me a job, gave me a family. The family Cody kept from me. I can't help but wonder if I was in love with the wrong brother all along. I was happy with Cody. I don't want that to ever be in question. But I *love* you. You're it for me."

Jet's head reeled. He'd never expected her to say all that let alone mean it all. She *did* mean it all, didn't she?

Looking into her shining blue eyes, his heart believed every word she said. And it almost brought him to his knees.

"I love you, Holly." He caressed her cheek.

She nodded, her face beaming with joy. "I love you so much, Jet."

He crushed her to him. *Thank You, Lord Jesus, for bringing her into my life. Thank You for her love.*

Holding her face in his hands, he searched her eyes before lowering his lips to hers. This time, he kissed her slowly, deliberately, savoring the taste of her lips, the softness matching her kind heart.

He would never forget this moment.

He would never take her for granted.

When he ended the kiss, he led her to the bench. They sat side by side, holding hands, looking into each other's eyes.

"We have a lot to talk about." He grew serious. He hadn't really thought this far ahead. It had seemed virtually impossible she would love him back. Now, how were they going to move forward? "I know you have a new life planned here. I'm sure you're excited about the job and reconnecting with your cousin." He gulped, afraid of what might come next. He didn't know how to work this out with her here and him in Wyoming. "I won't ask you to give it all up."

"You don't have to ask me." She beamed. "I want to give it all up."

"You do? But I thought you—"

"I don't. I don't even know what you were going to say, but I'm assuming it has something to do with starting over near Morgan and all that. I don't want it. I love her. It's been great reconnecting. But I belong in Sunrise Bend."

Were fireworks exploding over his heart? "You mean it?"

"I do."

What a relief!

"I can't wait to have you back. And Mom and Reagan will be so happy to hear you're returning." Then he frowned. "You do want to work with them, still, don't you?"

"Oh, yes. I loved working with them. I can't remember the last time I was allowed to have any input in marketing or the creative side of the ~~~iness. They gave me freedom, and they listened to my ideas. Do you think they still have room for me there?"

"Yes." He nodded a little too hard. This was all working out better than he'd ever imagined. "There's room. They want you."

Her smile chased away every other thing they needed to discuss. All he wanted to do was to stare into her eyes, hold her hand and sit next to her on this bench forever.

"What about the cottage?" she asked.

"It's yours. Well, for now."

She frowned. "What do you mean for now?"

He swallowed, not sure how much to say. "You're the one who told me life was short."

"I remember."

"I'm not trying to rush things, but I'm also not going to pretend I don't see you and Clara in the house I'm building."

"Really?"

"I wouldn't say it if I didn't." He squeezed her hand. "I wouldn't mind seeing a couple more kids in that house someday."

"I think you read my mind." She leaned in and kissed his cheek.

"What happens next?" he asked.

"First, I'm going to introduce you, properly this time, to my cousin. Then I guess I'll have to take my name off the waiting list for the apartment and call the store to let them know I won't be working there, after all."

"How soon do you want to go back to Sunrise Bend?"

"As soon as possible."

"Morgan, this is Jet. He's the cowboy I told you about, Cody's oldest brother." Holly was practically floating, she was so overjoyed. As soon as they'd returned to the apartment, Jet had taken Clara from Morgan, and her baby's smiles told her she was as delighted to see Jet as her mama was.

"It's great to meet you," Morgan said, shaking his hand. She reintroduced Cameron, who shook his hand, too.

Drake came up to Jet and tilted back his head. "I wanna be cowboy."

Holly laughed, and Jet crouched, keeping a tight hold on Clara. "Well, buckaroo, you'll have to come out to my ranch sometime. We'll have you on a horse before you can say boo."

Drake clapped his hands and started hopping around yelling, "Cowboy, cowboy."

"Looks like I'll be picking up a cowboy hat from the dollar store soon." Morgan pretended to groan. Then she looked from Holly to Jet and back to Holly. "Sooo…what's going on?"

Holly moved to Jet's side, and he slung his arm

over her shoulders as she wound her arm around his waist. "I'm moving back to Sunrise Bend."

Morgan's face fell, but she recovered quickly. "Can't say I blame you."

"I can never thank you enough for always being here for me, Morgan."

"Anytime." Her eyes glistened. "When do you think you'll be leaving?"

"Soon." Holly looked up at Jet. "Real soon."

The four of them talked for a while, then Morgan and Cameron took Drake to get ice cream.

"When do you think you can have everything packed?" Jet asked, sitting next to Holly on the couch.

"Two hours." She grinned. "I've been living out of a suitcase for weeks. All my stuff is still in my car."

"I took the whole week off."

"You?" She mocked horror as she placed her palm against her chest.

"Yes, me." He lifted his gaze to the ceiling. "I know, it's shocking. How would you feel about doing some sightseeing before we go back to Sunrise Bend?"

Her ears perked up. "Like where?"

"I don't know. I've never been to Salt Lake City." He curled a ribbon of her hair around his finger.

"It's right next door to Ogden." She clapped

her hands lightly. "Let's do it. And I've always wanted to visit Arches National Park."

"Me, too." He nestled her closer to him. "Let's make a list of all the things we can cram into the next week."

"Oh, yes! And we should make a list of all the other places we want to go, you know, on other vacations."

"I think you read my mind." He bent his head and kissed her. "I'll follow wherever you want to go."

"Something tells me we're going to have a lot of adventures."

One week later, Jet parked his truck in front of his cabin as Holly pulled her car up in front of the cottage. He got out, stretching both arms high to the sky. All was right with the world.

The weather had grown warm, finally. He'd ditched the jacket and felt comfortable in jeans and a T-shirt. This had been the best week of his life. And he couldn't wait to see Blaine, his parents and sisters in person.

He'd called each individually to tell them about him and Holly and their plans. Thankfully, they'd all whooped and hollered. No one had seemed put out by the news they were in love.

With easy strides, he approached Holly. "Hey

there, beautiful." He kissed her cheek. "Are you ready to see the family?"

"I am. Reagan told me she was literally having withdrawals from missing Clara so much, and your mom wants me back in the showroom Monday morning."

Jet took Clara out of her car seat and lifted her up before kissing her forehead. "Did you miss Grammy and Grandpa?" She blew a raspberry in response. Boy, he loved this little girl.

"Are you sure you don't want to relax for a while? Freshen up before heading over?"

"No. I want to see them now."

"Okay." He offered her his arm. "Let's do this."

They strolled up the lane to the main house. Inside, the entire family had gathered in the great room. As soon as they saw Holly and Clara, they swarmed her.

"We're so glad you're back." Reagan hugged Holly then plucked Clara out of Jet's arms. "I have a dozen new candle scents needing catchy names and labels. We're lost without you."

Holly looked a bit teary-eyed, but Jet figured it was inevitable. The woman truly didn't know how much they all valued her.

"Now there's a sight for sore eyes!" Mom came up to him, placed both hands on his cheeks and kissed him. "And you brought our Holly and Clara back with you." She turned to greet Holly.

Erica leaned in and whispered, "Smart move, Jet."

Then Blaine was in front of him, grinning. "I guess this means you're going to be riding my back again, huh?" He turned to Holly. "Tell this one the ranch ran like a fine-tuned machine while he was gone."

She gave Blaine a quick hug then turned to Jet with a cheeky grin. "The ranch ran like a fine-tuned machine while you were gone."

"I'm not taking your word for it," Jet joked. "If I went out there right now, would the bulls' feeder ring be in good shape?"

"It would."

"And the pastures—would the fence all be fixed?"

"They would." His dad's voice caught him off guard. Dad pulled him in for a hug, patting him on the back twice before letting him go. "The ranch is in tip-top shape, son. And I want to thank you for maintaining it so well. You stepped up when I needed you most. When the whole family needed you, really. I'm proud of you. And grateful."

Jet's throat couldn't squeeze any tighter. His dad rarely praised him or Blaine, so to hear those words was unexpected, something he'd hold on to.

"Thanks, Dad," he said gruffly. "Learned from the best."

He peeked at Holly—Erica was now holding Clara and talking to Holly and Reagan. The three women laughed about something.

Mom drifted back over to him. "You did good, Jet."

"God blessed me, that's all." He stared into her eyes, brimming with love and happiness, and he felt stronger than ever.

"God blessed us all. I'm glad you've realized what will make you happy. She'll make a great partner for you when you two are ready to take the next step."

The next step. He liked the sound of that. One thing at a time, though.

"So, Erica, what do we need to do in the next two weeks for this wedding to happen smoothly?" he asked.

"Well, for one, you need to help Jamie with the playlist. He's got the weirdest taste in music..."

"Come on, kids. I have two pans of lasagna in the oven. Let's eat."

As everyone headed to the kitchen, Jet pulled Holly aside. "Thank you. You brought a lot of happiness back to this family."

"All because of you, Jet."

"With you by my side, anything's possible."

"You and me together. I love you."

Epilogue

~❦~

This wasn't Jet's first wild-goose chase, and it probably wouldn't be his last.

"I'm telling you, she's going to love it." Reagan's insistent voice came through the phone. "Do not—I repeat, do not—even think about taking any advice from your idiot friends."

"As if I would." Jet steered the truck to the florist in town. "Randy and Blaine are bad enough with their ideas—I mean their hunting and fishing proposals are the dumbest things I've ever heard. But Mac, who is usually smart, was actually worse with his lassoing proposal."

"I shudder even thinking about it." Reagan made a sound of disgust. "Just get the flowers. Mom and I have the rest handled."

"Okay." He hung up and found a parking spot.

The past two months had been wonderful, busy and had him completely out of his element. First, Holly and Clara had settled right back into life on the ranch as if they'd never left. Second, Erica's wedding had been everything she'd dreamed of, and she'd officially moved out. He even missed her—not that he'd ever tell her that. Third, Tess and Sawyer had gotten married Saturday in a small ceremony. They'd hosted a reception at her ranch, and Jet had been honored to be a groomsman.

Holly had been his date, and all this wedding hoopla must have worn off on him, because he was proposing to Holly in a few hours. If his nerves didn't explode first.

Ten minutes later, he carried dozens of white roses to the truck and headed home. Mom and Reagan were finalizing the details at the candle shop, and Hannah Carr had convinced Holly to spend the day being pampered with her at the local salon.

He drove too fast all the way back, and the truck jolted to a stop in front of the shop. He carried the flowers and other items Mom had insisted on to the door.

As soon as he was inside, he stopped dead in his tracks. They'd dimmed the lighting, set up a table with a tablecloth and fine china. Romantic music played in the background. Naturally, candles were flickering everywhere.

"We've got it all set, hon." Mom bustled over,

carrying a candle box wrapped in a bow. "Open it. Just take off the lid."

He did, and nestled inside was a candle perfectly placed on a satin pillow. Its label read *Will You Be Mine?* Illustrations of two hearts and a ring completed it. He picked up the candle and unscrewed the lid.

There, on top, was Jet's grandmother's ring. The ring Cody had given to Holly. The ring she'd returned.

"Are you sure I shouldn't have gotten her a new ring?" he asked, setting the box down and massaging the back of his neck. "I don't want to remind her of Cody and…"

Reagan had joined them and was nibbling the tip of her fingernail.

"I think she's going to love this, Jet." Mom patted his arm. "If it wasn't for Cody, you never would have met her. This ring is part of your story. She'll want it."

"What do you think, Reagan?" he asked.

Her eyes widened. "I think Mom's right. But I also think you should offer to buy her a new one if she doesn't want this one."

"Good idea." He gave her a quick hug. "Okay, how much time do I have?"

"Not enough." Mom shooed him away. "We'll arrange the flowers. Go get dressed and get back here pronto."

Jet did as he was told and, within the hour, he was back in the candle showroom, listening to last-minute advice from Mom and Reagan, who were making his head spin. Thankfully, they finally left after he promised he'd text them the minute she said yes.

What if she didn't say yes?

He adjusted his cuffs and inspected everything. Supper was in the oven. The candle box with engagement ring was on the counter. Flowers were everywhere, letting off their sweet scent.

The door opened and Holly entered, looking like every one of his dreams come true.

When she saw him standing there, she took a step back. "Oh! I didn't see you. What are you doing here? Your mom insisted I come and check to see if she'd turned off the new melter in the back."

He took her in, from the top of her wavy blond hair to her rosy lips, the pretty dress skimming over her curves and stopping at the pink toenails peeking out of her high-heeled sandals.

"You are magnificent." He closed the distance between them and put his hands on her shoulders to kiss her cheek. "Come with me."

"Thank you." She blushed. "I feel kind of silly. Hannah wanted to try on dresses. She has another wedding to attend this summer, and she insisted I get this one and wear it home. It's so pretty, I couldn't say no."

"It's more than pretty." He had to clear his throat. "You take my breath away."

Her blush deepened.

"Why are you dressed up?" Her eyebrows drew together in the most adorable way. "I'd better make sure the melter is turned off before I forget."

"It's off." Keeping her hand in his, he led her to the table.

She finally seemed to notice her surroundings. "What are all these flowers—the table—what's going on?"

Caressing the back of her hand with his thumb, he felt a sense of calmness wash over him. This felt right. Holly was right—the right woman for him.

"Holly, we haven't been together long, but I know what I want. I've known it for a long time. I hope you feel the same way." He reached over for the box and handed it to her.

"What's this?" Her blue eyes glimmered with anticipation.

"Open it."

She lifted the cover off the box and gasped. Then she carefully took out the candle. "It's lovely. So romantic. Reagan must have designed this."

"Holly, you haven't left my mind since the minute I saw you. You took my leathery, scarred heart and made it beat again. I love you. I want to spend the rest of my life with you. I want to go on so many adventures we'll never stop talking about them." He bent on one knee. "Will you marry me? Say you'll be mine."

"Yes, yes!" She threw her arms around him, and he rose, kissing her.

"Look inside." He handed her the candle. He held his breath, watching her reaction as she took off the lid. Her eyes met his. "If the ring makes you uncomfortable for any reason, I'll take you to the jeweler with no questions asked. We'll pick out anything you want."

"No, Jet. It's perfect." Tears glistened in her eyes as he took out the ring and slid it on her finger. "I'll always be grateful for Cody. He gave me Clara. But he also led me to you. I love you with every bit of my heart."

"My heart is yours. All of it. Always."

"And forever."

* * * * *

*If you enjoyed this romance by Jill Kemerer,
pick up the first book in her
Wyoming Ranchers miniseries,*
The Prodigal's Holiday Hope.

Available now from Love Inspired Books.

Dear Reader,

I got the idea for this book after watching a show about a case of stolen identity. It made me think about other ways people can steal from each other, not physical things like money, but the experiences that shape them. I have so much sympathy for Holly, Jet and Cody. All three made mistakes, and all three turned to God to help them get back on track. God's good at that—making beauty from ashes.

It's terribly easy to feel like Holly—unimportant and tossed aside. But no matter what our circumstances, God loves us. We're important to Him. It's also easy to be like Jet and get wrapped up in the lie that we have to control everything around us. Holding on too tightly only causes us pain. Like Holly, we can remind ourselves, *This I know, God is for me*.

I hope you enjoyed this book. There are more romances coming for Jet's friends, and none of them will be smooth sailing! I love connecting with readers. Feel free to email me at jill@ jillkemerer.com or write me at P.O. Box 2802, Whitehouse, Ohio, 43571.

God bless you,
Jill Kemerer

Get 4 FREE REWARDS!

We'll send you 2 FREE Books plus 2 FREE Mystery Gifts.

Love Inspired books feature uplifting stories where faith helps guide you through life's challenges and discover the promise of a new beginning.

FREE
Value Over
$20

YES! Please send me 2 FREE Love Inspired Romance novels and my 2 FREE mystery gifts (gifts are worth about $10 retail). After receiving them, if I don't wish to receive any more books, I can return the shipping statement marked "cancel." If I don't cancel, I will receive 6 brand-new novels every month and be billed just $5.24 each for the regular-print edition or $5.99 each for the larger-print edition in the U.S., or $5.74 each for the regular-print edition or $6.24 each for the larger-print edition in Canada. That's a savings of at least 13% off the cover price. It's quite a bargain! Shipping and handling is just 50¢ per book in the U.S. and $1.25 per book in Canada.* I understand that accepting the 2 free books and gifts places me under no obligation to buy anything. I can always return a shipment and cancel at any time. The free books and gifts are mine to keep no matter what I decide.

Choose one: ☐ **Love Inspired Romance**
Regular-Print
(105/305 IDN GNWC)

☐ **Love Inspired Romance**
Larger-Print
(122/322 IDN GNWC)

Name (please print)

Address   Apt. #

City   State/Province   Zip/Postal Code

Email: Please check this box ☐ if you would like to receive newsletters and promotional emails from Harlequin Enterprises ULC and its affiliates. You can unsubscribe anytime.

Mail to the **Harlequin Reader Service:**
IN U.S.A.: P.O. Box 1341, Buffalo, NY 14240-8531
IN CANADA: P.O. Box 603, Fort Erie, Ontario L2A 5X3

Want to try 2 free books from another series! Call 1-800-873-8635 or visit www.ReaderService.com.

---

*Terms and prices subject to change without notice. Prices do not include sales taxes, which will be charged (if applicable) based on your state or country of residence. Canadian residents will be charged applicable taxes. Offer not valid in Quebec. This offer is limited to one order per household. Books received may not be as shown. Not valid for current subscribers to Love Inspired Romance books. All orders subject to approval. Credit or debit balances in a customer's account(s) may be offset by any other outstanding balance owed by or to the customer. Please allow 4 to 6 weeks for delivery. Offer available while quantities last.

Your Privacy—Your information is being collected by Harlequin Enterprises ULC, operating as Harlequin Reader Service. For a complete summary of the information we collect, how we use this information and to whom it is disclosed, please visit our privacy notice located at corporate.harlequin.com/privacy-notice. From time to time we may also exchange your personal information with reputable third parties. If you wish to opt out of this sharing of your personal information, please visit readerservice.com/consumerchoice or call 1-800-873-8635. **Notice to California Residents**—Under California law, you have specific rights to control and access your data. For more information on these rights and how to exercise them, visit corporate.harlequin.com/california-privacy.

LIR21R2

THEIR SECRET COURTSHIP
by Emma Miller

Resisting pressure from her mother to marry, Bay Stutzman is determined to keep her life exactly as it is. Until Mennonite David Jansen accidentally runs her wagon off the road. Now Bay must decide whether sharing a life with David is worth leaving behind everything she's ever known...

CARING FOR HER AMISH FAMILY
The Amish of New Hope • by Carrie Lighte

Forced to move into a dilapidated old house when entrusted with caring for her *Englisch* nephew, Amish apron maker Anke Bachman must turn to newcomer Josiah Mast for help with repairs. Afraid of being judged by his new community, Josiah tries to distance himself from the pair but can't stop his feelings from blossoming...

FINDING HER WAY BACK
K-9 Companions • by Lisa Carter

After a tragic event leaves widower Detective Rob Melbourne injured and his little girl emotionally scarred, he enlists the services of therapy dog handler Juliet Newkirk and her dog, Moose. But will working with the woman he once loved prove to be a distraction for Rob...or the second chance his family needs?

THE REBEL'S RETURN
The Ranchers of Gabriel Bend • by Myra Johnson

When a family injury calls him home to Gabriel Bend, Samuel Navarro shocks everyone by arriving with a baby in tow. His childhood love, Joella James, reluctantly agrees to babysit his infant daughter. But can she forget their tangled past and discover a future with this newly devoted father?

AN ORPHAN'S HOPE
by Christina Miller

Twice left at the altar, preacher Jase Armstrong avoids commitment at all costs—until he inherits his cousin's three-day-old baby. Pushing him further out of his comfort zone is nurse Erin Tucker and her lessons on caring for an infant. But can Erin convince him he's worthy of being a father *and* a husband?

HER SMALL-TOWN REFUGE
by Jennifer Slattery

Seeking a fresh start, Stephanie Thornton and her daughter head to Sage Creek. But when the veterinary clinic where she works is robbed, all evidence points to Stephanie. Proving her innocence to her boss, Caden Stoughton, might lead to the new life she's been searching for...

HARLEQUIN SELECTS COLLECTION

19 FREE BOOKS IN ALL!

From Robyn Carr to RaeAnne Thayne to Linda Lael Miller and Sherryl Woods we promise (actually, GUARANTEE!) each author in the Harlequin Selects collection has seen their name on the *New York Times* or *USA TODAY* bestseller lists!